CLAIRE AND THE QUARTET BOOK 10

Claire and the dogs.

Lin Joy

Copyright © 2024 Lin Joy

All rights reserved

The characters and events portrayed in this book are fictitious. Any similarity to real persons, living or dead, is coincidental and not intended by the author.

No part of this book may be reproduced, or stored in a retrieval system, or transmitted in any form or by any means, electronic, mechanical, photocopying, recording, or otherwise, without express written permission of the publisher.

Daddy feeds the blackbird,
Mummy feeds the wren,
and tells the tiny bird
to hurry back again.
Grandpa feeds the sparrow,
Grandma feeds the crow,
and that is nice to know.

Lin Joy

CHAPTER 1
The Big Announcement

One day, just after the evening meal, Mr Goodyard entered the kitchen and asked all members of staff, and Claire, to assemble in the sitting room, for she was going to make an important announcement. "This sounds rather ominous," said Mrs Low, the cook, when Mrs Goodyard left the kitchen.

"I do hope we don't have to get split up," said Claire.

"I do hope not," said Bella, the maid."

"Let's go to the sitting room where we'll find out our fate," said Claire mum, who was the housekeeper and in overall charge. It was unusual for Mrs Goodyard to even enter the kitchen, never mind having a full staff meeting in the sitting room. With trepidation they made their way to the sitting room. Claire's mum knocked at the door and entered. Sitting there alone was Mrs Goodyard with a worried look on her face. They were invited to sit down and then Mrs Goodyard spoke.

It appeared that the company which Mr Goodyard was working for was expanding their operations, and was setting up a branch abroad. Mr Goodyard was heading the team to set up the new branch of the company and they would be departing at the end of the week.

The good news was that the Goodyards were to be replaced by another couple, and everyone in the room would keep their jobs. Mrs Goodyard showed them a few pictures of the new couple that she had on her laptop. The staff then returned to the kitchen feeling slightly less anxious than when they left. They were all sad to hear that the Goodyards were leaving, but were glad that none of them would lose their jobs. "I think our jobs are safe for now, but the new couple may well want to bring about changes," said Mrs Low. All eyes in the room turned and looked upon Mrs Low. She was the most experienced person in the room having spent more than forty years in domestic service, and what she said was to be taken seriously. "There will be changes," predicted Mrs Low. "The woman in the photos had a proud look. Yes indeed there are going to be changes." Little did anyone in the room know that the changes would be worse than anyone had envisaged.

"Well let's serve our own dinner now and ask Claire to say grace," said Claire's mum.

CHAPTER 2
The New Mistress

The changes did take place. Mr and Mrs Goodyard left and the new occupants Mr and Mrs Toeser moved in. Mr Toeser was now the CEO for the company in the UK and Mrs Toeser, who had nothing to do with the business side of the company would now run the house, and be the hostess for the dinner parties that she would have to arrange. It seemed all very simple to her, and why Claire's mum was there she just could not understand. Nevertheless, on her first day at the house she introduced herself to staff in the sitting room and told them to continue working as before.

The first dinner party to take place was to be on Friday evening, just a few days away. It had been arranged by Mrs Goodyard and Claire's mum, mainly Claire's mum, and all that now had to be done was for the guests to arrive. It was a great success and as usual, Claire's mum gave all the credit for the success to the mistress of the house, which was now Mrs Toeser. She never spoke of her own part in the success. That is what etiquette demanded, and Claire's mum followed the etiquette.

A few days after the successful dinner party, Mr Toeser one morning, just as he was about to set off for the office, asked his wife to set up another dinner party in about a fortnight's time. She was only too happy to do so. "If Mrs Goodyard can arrange a successful dinner party, so can I," said to herself. "I don't see any point in that woman," and here she was referring to Claire's mum, "in being here at all. She is being paid good money just for being here and besides she has a child here just taking up room with her pets and her very presence. No, the pair of them will just have to leave."

That very hour she summoned Claire's mum into her sitting room where she told her that they no longer required her help. She gave her a month's notice, but anxious to get rid of her as soon as possible, she gave her a month's wages and told her to leave as soon as possible. Claire's mum was more worried about how her daughter, Mrs Low and Bella would take the news than losing her own job. Having worked just a few days with Mrs Toeser she had found her to be a rather unpleasant person. The way she treated the staff was anything but respectful, and the way she complained about Claire and her pets was just so disgusting, for after all she was talking to Claire's mother.

As soon as she was back in the kitchen the rest of the staff and Claire could sense that there was something amiss. Mrs Low did not hold back, neither did Bella. They left the kitchen, and went to Mrs Low's bedroom to decide what to do next. They all agreed that they no longer wanted to work for this awful woman, so Mrs Low and Bella paid a visit to Mrs Toeser's sitting room, knocked at the door and entered. Mrs Toeser looked up from writing on her computer, looking rather annoyed that she had been interrupted. Mrs Low and Bella now wanted even more to leave her employment. They had no intention in resigning and what they wanted was to be sacked, and receive their final pay cheque.

"What's this I hear about you sacking the housekeeper?" demanded Mrs Low with arms folded defiantly.

"How dare you speak to me like that! You're just a cook with that useless house maid standing next to you. You're both fired."

Both Mrs Low and Bella then pleaded with her not to fire them, but this fixed Mrs Toeser's resolve more firmly. She was enjoying the power she had to ruin their lives. "Now get out," she yelled. They turned and left.

"I think that went quite well Bella, so what do you think?" said a very pleased Mrs Low.

"That was you at your best Mrs Low. I think she'll be paying us a visit quite shortly," said Bella, as they went back into the kitchen. Mrs Low smiled.

Fifteen minutes later another door burst open, the kitchen door, and someone walked in. It was Mrs Toeser still in a rage. She had printed out and signed letters of dismissal for each of them, which she now flung down on the kitchen table along with their pay cheque. "I want you all out of here as soon as you can and within a week. I still expect you to cook and do the housework, and don't ever expect a reference from me. Your behaviour has been an absolute disgrace, and as for that girl and her pets, well I never want to see that lot again. Remember now, out by a week." So saying she turned on her heels and left, slamming as hard as she could, the door behind her.

Claire's mum had a super smile on her face and gave Mrs Low and Bella the thumbs up for a good job done. She put her index finger to her lips and then looked over at Bella and nodded. Bella knew just what to do. "What am I going to do?" she yelled at the top of her voice. All those in the kitchen knew that Mrs Toeser had gone no further than a few steps from the other side of the kitchen door. She would be enjoying the misery she thought she had wrought. "I have lost my job and it's all your fault, Mrs Low. Just look at the mess we are in," screeched Bella, trying her best not to burst out laughing.

"It's not my fault," protested Mrs Low. "It's that girl and her stupid pets. It's her fault."

"How dare you talk about my daughter like that," yelled Claire's mum, with another giant smile on her face. Claire then burst out crying and the dogs started to bark in the scullery. Claire calmed them down and then they all listened. Mrs Toeser had heard enough. They could hear her footsteps, on the varnished wooden floor of the corridor walking away.

CHAPTER 3

Time to Leave

It was now time for the staff to have their breakfast. Mrs Low said grace and asked for God's help throughout the day. As they sat around the kitchen table they discussed their future prospects. "It was just me who Mrs Toeser wanted to get rid off," said Claire's mum, "but although I should not really say this, I'm glad you also got fired." Both Bella and Mrs Low really did not know what to say. Bella glanced at Mrs Low with an anxious look, hoping she would say something, and she promptly obliged.

"Even if that awful woman had not sacked you we would have left," said Mrs Low, with her eyes upon Claire's mum. "No one I know around here would want to work for a woman like that." At that very moment Claire coughed, put her index finger to her lips and nodded to the kitchen door. It was a signal that Mrs Toeser was approaching. Mrs Toeser was tiptoeing along the corridor, so she could get undetected to the kitchen door, where she could listen in to what was being said. She knew she had been rash to sack Mrs Low and Bella, for being such a proud person she could just not help herself, but now that she had to arrange a dinner party on her own she had second thoughts. As for Claire's mum, she certainly believed, rather mistakenly, she had no need of her, while a cook and a house maid were essential.

Mrs Toeser listened through the door but heard nothing, so she took it as a sign they also were regretting what had just occurred. She was now going to show Mrs Low and Bella just how nice she could be, so she entered the kitchen and gave them both a kind smile, then told them they could stay.

"We prefer to leave," was all Mrs Low said, as she watched the kind smile disappear from the face of Mrs Toeser to be replaced by a scowl of utter hatred, that made Bella want to leave there and then. Mrs Toeser turned and left, banging the door behind her.

"Mrs Flowers should be up by now," said Claire. "I'll go and see if she will let us store our furniture in her stable until we find another post." Claire was keen to start the process of leaving, and just a few minutes later was found to be at Mrs Flowers' front porch ringing the bell. Jennifer, who had dropped in at Mrs Flowers' on her way to school, answered the door followed by Mrs Flowers. Claire told them both the news which caused them to be rather upset. Jennifer left for school and Mrs Flowers took Claire to her sitting room. "I have come to ask if we can keep our furniture in your stable until my mother finds another job?" asked Claire.

"Of course you may," said Mrs Flowers. "Now you go and tell the others in the kitchen that they are my guests until they find a new position. Things moved along quickly. Eleanor's father came with his van and moved the furniture, not into the stable, but into Mrs Flowers' safe lock up.

CHAPTER 4
Mrs Flowers to the Rescue

By the end of the day, Mrs Low and Bella had received a very good offer from a lady in a large house just a few houses away. She was about to give birth and was looking for a cook and a maid. It was no surprise, for Mrs Low had the reputation of being the best cook in the district. As for finding an appointment for Claire's mum, well that was turning out to be slightly more difficult. There was no demand for a live-in housekeeper in the district. Mrs Flowers, wanting to help her friends, joined in the search. She had learned from a friend about a son who was looking for a live-in housekeeper to look after his elderly mother. Unfortunately, the elderly lady, who had the reputation of not being an easy person to get on with, had recently sacked several housekeepers.

Mrs Flowers told Claire's mum about the job offer expecting her to decline it without hesitation. She talked it over with her daughter and they both prayed about it. Even though it may turn out to be like jumping from the frying pan into the fire, they both came to the conclusion that it was worth a try. "The poor woman may need our help," said Claire's mum, when she told Mrs Flowers that they would accept the challenge.

Claire's mum then had to make terms with the son, who would be doing the hiring. She had no intention of accepting the job if the terms were unsatisfactory. The first thing she obtained was an assurance that Claire could bring her pets. When the son heard that there was a hen, a rabbit and two dogs, he told them that Claire could have the use of an old empty hut along with a number of smaller huts plus an unused hen house thinking, hoping that might just persuade her to take the job. After some hard negotiations she accepted the job offer. The deal was put in writing and signed by them both.

Just a few days later, they said their goodbyes then it was the time to depart. Mrs Low and Bella were driven to their new home by Mrs Flowers, while Claire and her mum went in another, driven by the reliable Sid. The only things they took with them were their clothes, along with Claire's pets and, of course, Claire's chair along with that of her mother.

CHAPTER 5

From the Frying Pan into the Fire

It was a short journey for Claire and her mum to their new home compared to some of the similar journeys they had taken in the past. When they were almost at their destination, they branched off the main road onto a road that climbed up over a hill that led to a village on the other side of the hill. They had not gone far when they spotted the entrance to their new home with a driveway up to the mansion. Now Claire's mum had been given the phone number of Mrs Sipps, so she rang the number to tell her they had arrived. Sid then drove the van up the driveway to the porch at the front of the mansion, where stood an elderly lady dressed all in black waiting for them.

Claire's mum introduced herself and her daughter. Mrs Sipps looked Claire and her mother up and down and then spoke. "I really don't want you here at all," she told them, after her inspection. "I would prefer if you would just leave right now," she said, and paused, while giving them both another look of disapproval.

Claire's mum felt what Mrs Sipps was saying was

all fake, and that she really wanted them to stay. She was just doing this to establish her authority over them. Her son had hired them, but she wanted to show them that she could fire them any time she liked, so they better do what she tells them and do it in the way she wanted it done. Claire's mum now felt sure that there was a but coming along the lines that out of the kindness of her heart she would give them a chance. She was spot on, for Mrs Sipps opened her mouth to speak.

However, Claire's mum was just too quick for her. "Very well," she said, "if you want us to leave, then we shall go right now." She looked over at Sid who nodded his approval. So all three of them descended the steps of the porch and Sid opened the passenger door of his van for them to climb in.

Mrs Sipps had been struck dumb. This was something she certainly did not expect. "Wait," screamed Mrs Sipps, who had at last recovered her voice. "I was just going to say you may stay if you want to. You can put your things in the gate house and you and your daughter can stay and sleep there. You can work in my house during the day. There is no need for your daughter to enter my house. The gardener's house, which is empty, is where she shall be staying."

"I think we shall just leave anyway," said Claire's mother quite defiantly. I stay and sleep in the house where I am housekeeper, and my daughter stays with me." Upon saying this she stepped into Sid's van followed by Claire.

"Very well, if that's the way you want it," shouted Mrs Sipps. "Both of you may stay in my house together. I was only trying to be kind."

Enough had been said. "If you show us the servants' quarters we shall leave our belongings there," said Claire's mum. "What time is lunch?" Mrs Sipps told them. "Very well lunch shall be served at the usual time. I will come and collect the menu from you when we have finished unpacking," and that was that, as far as Claire's mum was concerned.

CHAPTER 6

Getting Down to Work

Now Mrs Sipps' son had hired Claire's mum to look after his mother. He knew she was not looking after herself properly, for any time he went to visit her he would inspect the kitchen to find out what food was in the kitchen and fridge freezer. To his horror he would find cupboards packed full of tins and packets of crispy cereals. No fresh fruit or vegetables were to be found anywhere. Claire's mum's job was to remedy the situation. To fund things Mrs Sipps' son had given Claire's mum a debit card containing a modest amount of money that would be topped up when needed by the son. On her way to their new home Claire's mum had called into a supermarket and bought enough fresh food to feed them all for several days. She bought with her own card things to feed Sid. If Claire and her mother choose to eat the same food as Mrs Sipps, then her son would fund them also. He felt that would help to ensure that his mother would eat more healthy food in the future. To avoid any charges of fraud this had been put in writing and signed with a copy given to Claire's mum.

After they had unpacked Clare's mum went to the sitting room where she knocked at the door and was told to enter. She had come to discuss the menu for lunch. "I just cannot make up my mind whether to have fish today or an omelette," said Mrs Sipps. She thought about it for a minute keeping Claire's mum standing waiting for her to make up her mind. "Fish," she said at last. She then ordered some other things, then told Claire's mum to leave and get on with it, which she promptly did.

"Claire, please take her meal to the dining room, then go and tell her it is ready and waiting," said Claire's mum. So Mrs Sipps went to the dining room with Claire following and sat down at the head of the table where lay the covered tray.

"Come here child and take that tray back to the kitchen and tell your mother that I have cancelled the first menu of fish, and now I just want an omelette," said a very angry Mrs Sipps.

"But," cried Claire, "this is the omelette you just ordered and upon saying this she whipped off the tea towel revealing a very nice ready to eat omelette.

"But, but," stammered Mrs Sipps, it's not what I ordered so why is it an omelette

"You ordered fish," pointed out Claire, "but you have just told me you changed your mind and ordered an omelette, and here it is."

"But that was just a few minutes ago," said Mrs Sipps, and it will take you at least ten minutes to make an omelette. Then it dawned on her what happened. She shut her mouth instantly and said not a word. She had been outwitted. Claire left after saying she would return after Mrs Sipps had finished eating. She then went back to the kitchen where they had a very nice fish lunch along with Sid who then left. They were alone again with a cantankerous and uncooperative old lady, who was determined to make life for them as miserable as she could.

CHAPTER 7
Bells in the Night

Now Mrs Sipps had a plan, and that very night she carried it out. She in no way was going to concede defeat to, what she called, this ghastly cook and her even more disgusting child. When she assumed that all in the house would be fast asleep, Mrs Sipps used the bell pull which caused one of the hanging bells this time in the hall to sound, indicating that she was upstairs in her bedroom. That meant that someone had to go and see what she wanted, so Claire's mother went upstairs, and found she wanted another blanket for her bed, so she got a blanket out of the bedroom cupboard. After sorting things out she went downstairs to her bedroom.

Not long after that, when all should be asleep it happened again, so Claire's mum climbed the stairs once more only to find out that she wanted some dried apricots, which were to be found in a jar in the kitchen. Claire's mum left and went back to the kitchen. When Claire found out that Mrs Sipps wanted dried apricots, she went to the cupboard and took out a jar of apricots. "It is obvious she is doing this for revenge over the omelette, fish, incident," said Claire.

"You are so right, Claire, and now she is doing her best to try and annoy me," said Claire's mother. "I have no intention of going back up these stairs to supply her with the apricots, which her son bought for her, and has never eaten and would probably just spit out if she ever tried to eat one. She can sack me if she wishes, but I am not going back up these stairs tonight." She was adamant about that.

"You get back to bed Mum," suggested Claire, "and I will give her the apricots instead of you, and that should put an end to her stupid prank." Claire knew that this could recur all through the night until dawn, and she was not going to let her mother be treated like that. So up the stairs Claire went, knocked at the bedroom door and entered carrying the jar of apricots along with a pair of hygienic tongs.

"I didn't ask for you to bring the apricots," growled a very cross old lady, when her eyes fell upon Claire. She had been sitting up in her bed, waiting and expecting Claire's mum to enter the room. Claire just ignored her comment and made her way to the bedside where she opened the jar.

"Shall I take an apricot out the jar for you?" madam asked Claire.

"I love apricots," said Mrs Sipps, "but if you think that I am going to eat one after your mucky hand has touched you are sorely mistaken. Just take the jar and leave. I shall use the bell pull *when* I need something else," she said, with a smirk of triumph on her face, thinking she was being terribly clever. Claire was right, for it was now obvious that she intended to call for more attention throughout the night.

Claire acted immediately by taking an apricot out of the jar using the hygienic tongs, and held it in front of Mrs Sipps. She stared at Claire, but Claire stared right back at her. She was hoping to out-stare Claire, but that was not just going to happen. Mrs Sipps was the first to flinch. She snatched the apricot from off the hygienic tongs and took a tiny bite.

"You may go now," she told Claire, with a wave of her free hand.

"I had better wait to see if you want another one, don't you think so?" asked Claire.

"No, I don't think so," she yelled at Claire. "Get out," she screamed."

"Shall I leave the jar, madam before I go?" asked Claire, who was completely unruffled by Mrs Sipps' behaviour. There was no answer so Claire walked over and laid it on top of the bedside cabinet. "I shall just leave it here," said Claire, just in case you get a craving for one during the night. "It will save my mother from having to climb the stairs once more tonight." Mrs Sipps said not a word, but just ground her teeth and growled. Claire started to leave, while keeping alert, as she made her way to the door. She could hear the rustle of bed clothes and a quiet groan of pain from Mrs Sipps. Clair turned round to see the jar of apricots to leave the outstretched hand of Mrs Sipps and fly across the room towards herself. Claire knew how to catch a cricket ball, so the jar of apricots was an easy catch for her. Claire said nothing, but just walked over to the bedside cabinet and replaced the jar. She then left, closing the door gently behind her.

Claire then went to the scullery and collected a step ladder and some unused bedding she had brought for the dogs. She went up the ladder, muffled the offending bell and then settled down in her bedroom in her Chair, to read the Bible and say her prayers. The bell never rang again that night for Claire would have heard even a muffled ring. There was no need for Claire to muffle the bell that night or any night in the future, for Mrs Sipps had been caught out, and she had learned the lesson not to try a silly stunt like that ever again.

CHAPTER 8
A Very Short School Day

The day soon arrived when Claire had to start her new school. After feeding her pets, she set out alone on her journey wondering what lay ahead for her. As she lived on a hill she could look down and see the town below spreading out in all directions. It used to be a small town a mile or so from the foot of her hill, but as the population had grown the town had expanded and now houses were to be found closer to the hill. She could see the school in the distance, a large modern building that looked more like a factory than a school.

Claire, if she wanted, could catch the school bus which started at the other side of the hill and which would pick up pupils from small villages and farmsteads. However, Claire chose not to go by bus that day because she was tired of the bullying and nasty behaviour that she had experienced in the past while travelling on school buses. No she would go down the fields and across the river which would bring her to the streets nearest the school. She arrived at the school just before it opened. It was then a girl about the same age as Claire came up to her and introduced herself. "Hello," she said, with a big smile on her face "My name is Gwen. It's nice to meet you. May I ask if you are new to the school?"

"Yes, I am new," replied Claire, "and it's nice to meet you too, Gwen. My name is Claire." It was at that moment the bell rang.

"I'll have to run," cried Gwen. "I'll have to get to my class or I shall be in trouble. Unfortunately, I won't be able to see you at the morning interval as I practise on the piano, but I hope to see you at the canteen at lunch. By the way, that's the school office over there," she said, pointing it out. She then went to offer Claire two cards about the same size as a credit card. "Here is something you may be interested in," she said, with a hopeful smile on her face. Claire took hold of the cards and Gwen ran off to her first class of the day. Claire placed the cards in her pocket and set off for the school office, while wishing that there had been more time to talk to Gwen and find out about her piano playing.

As Claire made her way to the school office she was approached by a boy and girl about her own age wearing the school uniform. "Hello," said the boy. "I'm Ron, and this is my friend Florence. May I ask you if you are new to this school?"

"Yes, I am new, Ron. I'm Claire, by the way. It's nice to meet you and your friend Florence."

"I was wondering if we and our friends could help you find your way around your new school?" asked Ron.

"We are just a group of children from our Sunday School who go to this school," said Florence

"We know it can be a harrowing experience starting a new school, especially when you don't know anyone here," added Ron.

"That is a good idea. I must say I would like your help to settle in here and I thank you both." They chatted until they came to the main school entrance and then they had to go on their own ways. Before parting they told Claire they would try and see her again at the morning interval.

Claire had with her the letter from the school telling her when she had to report to the office. She joined the queue at the office counter, where you could communicate with the office staff. As she waited she took from her pocket both cards that Gwen had given to her. One was an invitation to the Sunday worship at a local church and the other card, which looked like it had been home made, was an invitation to the Sunday School.

After waiting about a quarter of an hour it was now Claire's turn to speak to the office staff. She handed in the letter to a young man and waited to find out what class she was in, and to be given a time table. That did not happen. "We don't have any information on you," said an older woman, who was now dealing with Claire's case. Claire knew what was about to happen next, for she had experienced such treatment before. They would do their best to humiliate her, by having her sit in the waiting area and then after several hours of sitting there send her to sit in the library until the end of the school day. They would make her feel unwelcome and hope she would go to another school in the town. "You will just have to wait until it's sorted out," said the older lady, with her eyes fixed upon Claire. She was going to say more, but Claire was having none of it.

"Splendid," said Claire, interrupting the chief secretary, and preventing her from saying another word. "I shall just return home now. Please contact me by post when you have sorted things out," announced Claire in a very competent tone of voice. Off Claire went, before anyone could stop her, heading for home.

As Claire headed for home she just had to smile. "What is the school going to do now?" she asked a pair of wood pigeons, that sat watching her from the top of a nearby tree. "Nothing," said Claire, replying on behalf of the pigeons. "If they send a truant officer, which they won't, then the officer would learn about the school's incompetence in not having made proper arrangements for me and probably give the school a ticking off for time wasting.

As Claire had plenty of time on her hands she decided to go to a charity which she passed on her way to school. It was actually the Vets Vets Vets charity shop, and as Claire was to find out the only one in the town. She was in luck, for the shop was open so she entered. "Shouldn't you be in school right now?" asked a lady, who was removing books from a box and adding them to the shop's book shelf.

"I am a new girl," replied Claire, "and just waiting to find out when to start." She looked around the shop and left.

CHAPTER 9

Claire's New Friend

Claire's mother was surprised when Claire turned up at the back door of the servants' quarters of the big house. Her mother took Claire's view of the situation, namely that Claire would stay away from the school until they received the letter with the new return date. For the rest of the morning Claire decided to explore the surroundings taking Big Dog with her, but she left Mitzy resting in her basket after her morning walk. There were many fields and woods nearby and at the bottom of the hill was the river. "Perhaps I may spot a squirrel, or an otter, or even a fox. "You never know," Claire said to Big Dog, as they set off to explore the nearest wood "I might even spot a badger although they prefer the dark nights, but you never know. Let's head off to the wood and see what we can find." When they came to the wood Claire put Big Dog on the lead, just in case he went chasing after a rabbit and got lost. When they got deep into the wood, with Claire now and again looking up into the trees hoping to spot a squirrel, she suddenly heard a boy's voice. "Hello," said the voice. Claire looked around and about, but there was no one to be found. Then there was a rustle of leaves in the bushes and out walked a boy about her own age. Big Dog strained at the lead hoping to go up to the boy and greet him with a friendly outstretched paw. "Why aren't you at school?" asked the boy.

"Why aren't you?" replied Claire. They both looked at each other and then they both burst out laughing. "My name's Claire," may I ask yours?"

"As you know I'm meant to be in school," said the boy, and said no more.

"I'm meant to be in school too, but I told you my name," said Claire.

"Good point, but you may have a valid excuse, whereas I don't."

"Good point," said Claire. They both smiled. "You win for I indeed have an excuse."

"Let's call it a draw," said the boy, as he stretched out his hand for Claire to shake, which she did not hesitate to do. "Well," he said, "I'm Alexander, but my friends call me Sandy."

"May, I call you Sandy too?" asked Claire.

"You certainly can," replied Sandy. Just for a second Claire was sure that he blushed.

"You must be wondering what I am doing here, Sandy." Claire began to tell her story, but Sandy interrupted her.

"Come with your big dog and sit on this tree trunk where we can talk. By the way, now we know each other's name, what is the name of your big dog?"

"Why! He's called Big Dog, of course."

"Of course he is," said Sandy, trying not to laugh.

They both sat down on the tree trunk. Big Dog came over and sat next to Sandy who patted him gently as he listened to Claire's story. When she had finished it was time for Sandy to return to his farm, for he had work to do.

CHAPTER 10
The Return to School

Eventually the letter from Claire's school arrived giving the date when Claire had to attend school. This time there were no delays. She was given a time table and a list of the classes she would be in. Claire soon was sitting in her first class of the day. The other pupils in the class showed little interest in the newcomer and things just continued as usual. The next class was however entirely different.

It was a physics class and Claire was looking forward to the lesson, as she queued up at the laboratory with the rest of the pupils. She got strange looks from some of the children for she seemed to be the only girl in the class. All the other physics rooms were full up and so this one was the only one available. The door opened and the pupils entered in single file, then went to their places except Claire. She made her way to the teacher's desk and presented herself to him. "We have a new member in the class," announced the teacher, when the class had settled down. "This is Claire," he said, as Claire stepped forward and smiled. The children were seated in rows of benches, with six in the first two rows, but just four in the back row. There were actually five rows of benches in the room, but as the class had a small number of pupils the teacher just used the first three rows which made it a lot easier to watch what was going on.

The physics teacher was called Mr Elder, who was in his early thirties and wore a white lab coat. "Now where are we going to sit you?" he asked himself, with a concerned look on his face, for this was now the first girl that they ever had in this class of sixteen boys.

Claire looked around the class of all boys. "I have never ever been in a class of just boys," said Claire to herself. "They may tease me, so I think I might just have to show them the correct way to treat a girl. What must it have been like to have been the first woman doctor, or the first woman engineer or missionary? Just such amazing women."

"Now all I have to do is to find where I am to place you, Claire," said Mr Elder.

Claire glanced over at Mr Elder after surveying the boys. "There are only four in the third row, Sir," she told him, hoping that might help him to solve his predicament as to where to place her. He was about to direct Claire to the third row when a boy put up his hand to ask a question.

"Yes, what is it you want to say, Frank?" asked Mr Elder.

"*Sir,* he snapped. "We don't want her. Our row always gets them for a week or so before they get moved into another class. It's not fair, *Sir*."

"Sir, she can sit in our row, that is if she wants to," another voice rang out, from a boy called Kenneth, who rose to his feet and gestured with his hand to point out the empty seat next to him.

The room burst out laughing, and even Mr Elder had to do his best not to laugh. Kenneth was the one in the class who was always asking why there were no girls in the class. There were no girls in the class, simply because when the science classes were made up, the group of sixteen boys had such dreadful marks, and were told they had to take a science class instead. The science that they would have to take was known among the children as stupid science, but the parents of the sixteen boys were having none of that nonsense, and insisted that their boys take physics, as they had requested.

Mr Elder, for a moment, just did not know what to say or do. He wanted to protect the young girl, who he believed by now must be getting terribly upset. He looked at Claire to see how she was taking the hostility from Frank. To his surprise he found she was smiling and was not letting this experience upset her in the least. "Claire, would you like to sit beside Kenneth?" asked Mr Elder, thinking she would firmly reject the offer and that would silence Kenneth in a better way than he could ever accomplish.

Claire knew just how to react. "I would *love* to sit beside Kenneth," said Claire, as she fixed her eyes on the boy and smiled at him. It has been said that some in the class even believed they saw her wink. Kenneth blushed and his face turned red. He started to shake and sat down.

Kenneth then, this time put up his hand, so Mr Elder let him speak. "Sir, I did not really mean that she should actually sit next to me, but was just suggesting that she could sit in the row." He was beginning to have cold feet, and the whole class knew it and started to burst out laughing once more.

CHAPTER 11
The Spiteful Teacher

It was then that the classroom door burst open and in strode the head of the physics' department, a certain Mr Toby with a scowl on his face. Now Mr Toby did not like Mr Elder one bit. In fact, he hated him. Both were about the same age, but that is all they had in common, except both were physics teachers. Mr Elder did his very best to help the children, whereas Mr Toby did his level best to help himself get promoted even further. There was no need to say much more. "What is going on in this class?" he demanded to know, while moving his arms and hands around in what looked to Mr Elder, as threatening gestures.

"Excuse me, Sir," called out Frank, "but we were just celebrating that we now have a girl in our class. You must admit it is a good thing for diversity and all that very important stuff." He had to hesitate just for a moment, for instead of using the word stuff, out of his mouth almost came the word rubbish, and what an awful mistake that would have been. "Claire can come and sit in our row if she would like. She would be most welcome," suggested Frank. Mr Toby was now very annoyed for he had entered the lab to chastise the physics teacher for allowing his class for making too much noise, but the school was all in favour of diversity so he could not really complain about the class celebrating, and besides Frank's father was a leading member of the School's PTA and had a lot of influence in the town. Mr Toby for the first time now realised he had made a big mistake by placing only boys in this physics class, for Mr Elder to teach. He just saw them as an uneducable group of boys that would give Mr Elder a hard time.

Mr Elder now wanted to take back control of his class again and out of the hands of the head of the physics department. "Would you like to go and sit in Frank's row?" he asked Claire, who had been standing at the front of the class waiting to find out where she was to sit.

"I would love to sit *beside* Frank," answered Claire, with a big grin, "but unfortunately for him, Kenneth asked first, so with your permission, Mr Elder, I shall go and sit next to Kenneth." This time she gave Kenneth a definite wink. Everyone in the class just gaped at Claire, as she picked up her bag, went to the front row, moved along the row until she came to Kenneth and sat down next to him, which caused Kenneth to nearly jump out of his skin with fright.

Mr Toby knew it was now time for him to leave the class, so he moved to the door, opened it, and instead of slamming it, he closed it gently and went back to his own room. Mr Elder beckoned to his own class to stay quiet. They too did not like Mr Toby very much, and were now on their very best behaviour. Mr Elder was concerned now for Claire, but he need not have worried, for Claire just sat on her stool quite happily waiting for the lesson to begin. He then looked at Kenneth, the very boy who would ask him nearly every time the class met, when they were getting a girl in the class.

"Are you all right Kenneth?" Mr Elder asked him. "You are looking rather flustered."

"I'm OK. Sir. Just cannot wait until the lesson will start." There was a snigger from the whole class.

"Well, that's the first time I have ever heard you say that! I wonder why?" said Mr Elder.

At the end of the lesson Claire thanked God in a silent prayer, for helping her through her first physics class. She also thanked God for those pioneering women who were an example to many young girls as to what could be accomplished. She felt joy in her heart and looked forward to the next physics lesson.

CHAPTER 12

Claire meets the Bullies

At the morning interval Claire met up with Ron and Florence. It was then they were approached by a gang of sinister looking older pupils.

"They have wasted no time in their business," said Florence, when she spotted them. "They will be wanting you to pay protection money. It's best that you pay. We pay."

"Why?" asked Claire.

"Well it's like this, Claire. If we don't pay something bad will happen, like a broken arm or leg.

"I really would advise you to pay," said Florence, in a tone that sounded like she was giving Claire very sound advice, and that Claire should be grateful to her for such advice.

Ron and Florence had intended to warn Claire more about the gang, but had not been quick enough, for that very gang were now almost next to them. The gang of extortionists expected easy picking from Claire when they saw her with the two of their clients. How mistaken they were.

"Who's your friend?" asked the gang leader,

when he arrived and was towering over the three children.

"None of your business," Claire told him. He growled and turned his eyes on Claire, which, by now, were nearly popping out of their sockets. Ron and Florence gasped at Claire's reply, which they both regarded as being rather foolhardy. The rest of the gang looked at their leader with the expectation that he would teach this little girl a good lesson. He stretched out both hands towards Claire in an effort to grab hold of the lapels on her school jacket, and lift her up off the ground, so they would be facing each other eye to eye. However, *the best laid scheme of mice and men often go awry,* and this was one of them. Claire grabbed both his outstretched hands and thrust him to the ground. There he lay on his back, looking up at Claire with his mouth foaming and his podgy face as red as a tomato.

His gang members gasped with unbelief at what had just happened and stared at their leader with open jaws. He suddenly jumped to his feet and rushed towards Claire with fists flying. Claire had already summed him up to be a phoney. He was out of shape, slow and lumbering, unable to strike a blow. He was all show. His hairstyle, the way he could distort his features and his overall appearance, were used to scare others, but when it came to action he was quite useless. Claire got hold again of both his hands and then held him at arms length as he tried to kick her. "Just leave," ordered

Claire, and pushed him away, but he did not take her advice and came rushing at her once again. This time Claire just side stepped him as he made a dive at her, causing him to hit the ground on his stomach. He rolled himself round and looked into Claire's eyes.

"You're in big trouble," he spat out, in a very threatening voice, while wagging his finger at what he regarded just as a little girl. Claire grabbed hold of his hand, then pulled him up on his feet. "Take him away," Claire instructed his gang members, but they turned their backs on their humiliated leader and left. There he stood for a moment all alone before slouching away. When he had gone out of sight Claire turned and looked at Florence and Ron. They stood there fixed to the spot both with a terrified look upon their faces.

Claire then said a short prayer of thanks to God for her deliverance. "Bye the way." said Claire, addressing the two children, "what is the food like in the canteen?" It was as if they never heard a word that Claire had just uttered. No one spoke until Ron at last opened his mouth.

"We better be going now, Florence," he said, as he took his friend by the arm and left without even a glance at Claire. Claire was all alone once again.

CHAPTER 13
The Canteen Incident

When the bell rang Claire made her way to her next class. She kept a low profile and things went smoothly for her. The school was used to the comings and goings of pupils for many of the parents had temporary jobs in the town. The lunch break could not come quickly enough for Claire, who was looking forward to meeting her friends, Florence and Ron, once more, little knowing how disappointed she would end up.

When the class ended, Claire went to the canteen and joined the queue where she soon spotted her friends, near the front. Soon she had selected her meal and paid for it, and holding the tray in her hands she looked around for Florence and Ron. She spotted them sitting facing each other and went over to join them. Ron spotted Claire, but looked the other way. He must have told Florence of Claire's presence, for she turned and quickly glanced at Claire then turned away. Claire stood and waited hoping one of them would come and help her with her tray, or at least beckon to come and join them. Her heart sank for she now knew the truth, and that was they were deliberately ignoring her. They would deny her and claim that they never knew her.

Claire looked around for somewhere else to sit. There at the window, at the most desirable table, sat the gang leader who Claire had just humiliated that very morning. After what had happened at the morning interval, it surprised Claire greatly to see the gang members sitting with him. He seemed to be in a heated conversation with them, which made Claire think he was making excuses for what had happened just a few hours ago. Claire, with her acute hearing ability, walked slowly towards their table while listening to what they were saying. Her assumptions proved to be right. The gang leader was indeed trying to make out that he was still fit to lead them, while insisting he alone in the school could collect the vast amounts of protection money that they all enjoyed so much.

When Claire got up close to their table she stood and looked at them. They looked like such a sad bunch, the very type of youths that would rob from children. "Hello." said Claire, in a tone and volume for not only the gang could hear, but also for the other tables around to take note. Those facing the window turned round and those on the other side looked up.

"It's her," said one of them, who had turned round and was pointing at Claire. He, being the closest to Claire, looked around the canteen and noticed the teacher supervising the hall was dealing with someone in the queue, so he decided to act thinking all was clear and he would not be caught. He was emboldened, so when Claire drew close enough, he turned round and took a swipe at her, but missed, for Claire saw it coming as if in slow motion. He was hoping to knock the tray out of her hand so it would land on the floor, and the whole hall would give that well known sneering cheer when a plate smashed. However, it was he himself who was humiliated for Claire got hold of the back of his chair and gave it one might pull, and let go so that the chair was sliding away from the table on just two of its legs. The chair then toppled over leaving him still in it, but now lying on the floor looking up at the ceiling. Claire laid her tray down on a nearby table and bending down stretched out her hand offering to pick the youth up from the floor. To her surprise he took hold of her hand allowing Claire to lift him back on his feet. She then picked up the chair and sat the very dazed youth back into it, and pushed him back into his place at the table. Most in the hall had just seen what had happened, but there was an eerie silence as if nothing had occurred. Next she sat down at the empty table where she had left her tray and said grace in a quiet voice. The thugs heard her and out of their mouths flowed the vilest remarks about her that she had ever heard.

CHAPTER 14

A Friendly Face

It was when she had finished praying she heard a girl's voice which she recognised immediately. She looked up and there stood her friend Gwen holding her tray.

"Hello to you too, Gwen," said Claire, with a big smile.

"May I sit with you?"

"Oh yes, please do," replied Claire.

"I was not looking out for you and here you are," said Gwen. "I thought you were absent. Sometimes I'm absent too. That is when I am needed to help at home."

"I wasn't really absent," said Claire, and explained to her friend what had happened.

"So today is the day that you are starting school?"

"Yes it is, and things have gone well except at the morning interval a gang of extortionists wanted me to give them protection money. I refused, and told them to get lost," said Claire.

"Well done!" exclaimed Gwen. "I wish I had been there to see that. I was asking my music teacher if I could bring my new friend to watch me practising my piano playing. Was it that lot sitting over there with that thug who tried to punch you just a moment ago?

"Yes it is," replied Claire. "That is why I'm keeping an eye on them. They will try to harm me and also any of my friends. I have lost two friends already."

"Is that these two you keep looking at over there," asked Gwen.

"Yes, but never mind about them, they are just fair weather friends," said Claire, "but do tell me more about your piano playing in the school."

"Well," said Gwen, pleased that Claire had taken an interest in her playing, "Miss Beaven, my music teacher, lets me practise in her classroom at the morning interval and at lunch time. I shall be going back there after I have finished eating. Would you like to join me?"

"I would love to," replied Claire. She said that not to disappoint Gwen, but she really wanted to.

The two girls enjoyed their meal, but of course, all the time with Claire keeping a watchful eye on two tables in the canteen, one being that of the thugs almost next to hers, and the other where Ron and Florence were sitting with what appeared to be their friends. Never once did they glance in her direction. Claire was now a persona non grata, according to their way of thinking.

Claire and Gwen left the canteen together and on the way to Miss Beaven's room. Claire never asked Gwen whether or not she had paid the gang any protection money, for Claire reckoned it was none of her business, and that if Gwen wanted to tell her then that was up to Gwen.

CHAPTER 15
The Music Teacher

When they arrived at Miss Bevan's room they had to wait for her appearance. Soon she arrived and opened the door. "I see you have brought a friend," she said.

"I just wanted to ask you, if you are sure it's OK if Claire can please stay and hear me play?" Miss Bevan.

"*Of course,* Claire may stay," said Miss Bevan, as she looked at the young girl standing next to Gwen. She kept her eyes on Claire for just a second or two longer than necessary, thinking that she may have seen her before.

"Are you new to the school?" asked Miss Bevan.

"Yes I am, Miss."

"Well I hope you will enjoy your time here."

"I think I shall Miss, for I have made a new friend already." Miss Bevan smiled, and then went to her desk to do some paperwork, leaving Gwen to practise. Claire sat down and listened and was very impressed by Gwen's ability.

A quarter of an hour before classes would commence Miss Bevan rose and went over to

Gwen, to commend her for her playing. Usually it was only a few minutes before classes started that she would end Gwen's practice, but that day she wanted to find out more about Claire, not knowing really why. "Well, what do you think, Claire?"

"Gwen plays remarkably well, Miss," answered Claire. Gwen, who was still sitting at the piano, could not help smiling when she heard Claire's verdict on her playing

"Do you play the piano too, Claire?" asked Miss Bevan, as she glanced over at Claire sitting there in her class room. Once again she had that funny feeling she had seen Claire before, a little girl sitting alone at the front of a room with empty chairs arranged behind her back.

Miss Bevan had just asked Claire a question and Claire would now have to answer. "Yes Miss, I do play the piano." Then came the question she dreaded.

"Would you like to play for us now, Claire?" asked Miss Bevan, while glancing at the now vacated piano. Claire gazed up at Miss Bevan with her big round eyes and for a moment froze. If she played much better than Gwen, Claire felt that could humiliate her new friend, and if she pretended to play badly she felt she would be lying to Miss Bevan. Then suddenly she found just what to say.

"I think it's best for me not to play, Miss, for I would be comparing myself to Gwen, and we know they say comparisons are odious.

"Oh, do play for us, Claire," begged Gwen. "I'm

dying to hear you play," and so saying, she rose from the piano stool, went over to Claire and dragged the reluctant Claire over to the piano where she planked her down on the stool. There she sat at the piano wondering what on earth she would do next, so she looked over for help from Miss Bevan. Miss Bevan looked at Claire sitting alone on the piano stool when again those strange, forgotten but familiar sensations once again flooded into Miss Bevan's mind. Her vision came back of Claire sitting with empty chairs at her back, but this time the chairs filled by members of an orchestra. "You're Claire," Miss Bevan suddenly cried, while pointing her finger in Claire's direction. Gwen thought for a moment that her teacher had all of a sudden taken a funny turn, but Claire knew better. "She knows who I am," she said to herself, and sighed.

Miss Bevan, still with her eyes on Claire, realised she had perhaps made a mistake in unmasking Claire in this manner. "Claire, were you wanting to keep it a secret about your successful performances?"

"Not really," answered Claire, as she looked at Gwen, who appeared to be bewildered about what on earth the two of them were referring to. I was going to tell you and Gwen, but at the appropriate time, for right now it would have looked like I was just boasting." Gwen looked even more perplexed at what was going on.

"Claire, would you like me to tell Gwen? It would

not look like boasting if I tell her." Claire said not a word, but just nodded her approval. So Miss Bevan went on to relate to Gwen the story of Claire's success as a concert pianist. "I was there at Claire's debut when Claire replaced a world renowned virtuoso pianist at a concerto conducted by Sir Robert Buchanan," said Miss Bevan, when she finished her story about Claire.

As soon as Gwen realised that Miss Bevan had finished speaking, she ran to Claire and gave her what could only be called a super hug. "Is it really true, Claire?" asked Gwen, as she now took a step back so she could look Claire in the eyes. How wonderful! Isn't it wonderful that we have Claire here in our school. Isn't it marvellous?"

"Yes it is, Gwen, and I think you one day will become a concert pianist just like Claire. That's why I let you play the piano here whenever you can."

"Thank you," said Gwen. "I would love to be in the music Club after school," said Gwen, but I'm needed at home to help. Do you really think I could become a concert pianist, Miss?"

"Yes I do, Gwen."

"If I made some money that could help me go to university and study science and become like Madame Curie," said Gwen, very enthusiastically.

Miss Bevan at that point looked over at Claire to find out how she was reacting. Both knew that Gwen had no chance at going to university due to her frequent absences. For a moment both felt slightly cast down, but for Claire it was only for a moment and she ended up smiling once more. At that point the bell rang. Time for class now," said Miss Bevan, "and don't worry Claire, I shan't tell anyone about what we know."

"And I shan't either," said Gwen, as the two children left the room.

"Thank you, Miss," said Claire.

Several days later when Claire met up with Gwen in the canteen, she noticed her friend was looking rather forlorn. "I have just learned that Miss Bevan received the news this morning, that she had been promoted to the head of music in a school miles away from here. It is where her mother and father stay. I'll be so sorrowful to see her go, Claire."

"So shall I," said Claire sympathetically, for Gwen now would have no access to a piano.

"I don't expect her replacement, whoever it may be, will let me practise at the intervals. What do you think, Claire?

"I agree," said Claire reluctantly.

That Friday was Miss Bevan's last day at the school, Gwen and Claire bought a card and signed it and handed it to Miss Bevan. She thanked and urged Gwen to continue to study the piano.

CHAPTER 16

The Chase

The day wore on and Claire was soon back in a class where the pupils acted as if she did not exist. At the end of the school day Claire headed for home taking the same route across the rickety bridge at the fast flowing river. She knew she had been followed for when she was climbing the hill to her home she had glanced back and spotted a couple of youths watching her.

When she got to the top of the hill she hid and watched to see what they were up to, and found they had stopped following her. That night Claire sat in her chair and charged herself, while she contemplated the affairs of the day. She was convinced that her adversaries would be looking for instant revenge and would want to restore their reputation for being tough and ruthless among their gang of collectors. "They will probably set out to break my arm or leg, most likely my arm, so when later on that week I walk into the canteen with my arm in a plaster, I shall be a warning to those who dare to challenge their authority.

Next day Claire stayed on the alert from the moment she left the house. "They followed me yesterday on my journey home," said Claire to herself, as she made her way down the hill heading for the school. "Yesterday they watched me going up the hill then left, so I don't think that they will attack me now, but I think they will on my homeward journey," reasoned Claire.

That day at school Florence and Ron completely ignored Claire. She understood, for she knew that anyone that associated with her was in danger from the thugs. Claire was disappointed with them, but not surprised and wondered what she would do if she was in their place.

At the canteen that day Claire sat close to the gang demanding money with menaces, in short the extortionists. They kept looking at Claire all the time while sneering, smiling and whispering. That told Claire all she needed to know.

It did all happen on her way home. The attack started as soon as she left the street near the hill and stepped onto the meadow. Up drove a jeep and out jumped the gang leader and his younger brother from the school along with the driver who Claire took to be one of their older brothers. "I found out that they have two older brothers, so the other one must already be in the meadow or at the hill," said Claire to herself. She set off running away from them keeping a safe distance, but a distance to give them the hope of catching her. The whole place was deserted except for a crow sitting on a nearby tree. If it were to look down from its perch at the top of the tree, it would just see three youths running after a little girl, who was heading for the bridge across a nearby raging river. The rickety bridge, the name Claire had given to it, had been built at the narrowest part of the river so costing less to build, but the narrow part of the river was where the river flowed the fastest.

Claire turned and looked at the three of her pursuers. They were completely unfit and were already panting and puffing, so they had no chance of catching her. "Why do they keep chasing me towards the bridge?" Claire asked herself. It was at that moment she spotted a movement at the far side of the bridge. She had seen a head pop up from under the bridge and then disappear from view. She now knew the answer to her question. "That must be the fourth brother waiting there to attack me and throw me into the river," said Claire. It was the fourth brother, but for the rest of her reasoning, oh how wrong she had been.

CHAPTER 17
The Tragedy

Claire had no intention of falling into their trap, so when she was just about to reach the bridge she moved to the left of the bridge, and leapt across the river. She was not hurt, but she made out as if she had damaged her ankle. She now expected the fourth brother to appear and attack her.

The three brothers ran even faster to the bridge wanting to be the first to attack the injured girl. Claire was at their mercy, well so they believed. When they reached the middle of the bridge suddenly there was a loud thud and the bridge started to collapse. Bits of wood went flying everywhere and a cry of horror came from below the bridge as a large splinter of wood struck the head of the fourth brother knocking him into the raging waters below.

The fourth brother had attacked the main wooden support of the bridge with one mighty blow from his sledge hammer, unaware that by doing so he had sealed his own demise and those of his brothers. He had seen Claire running for her life, as fast as she could, away from his brothers. He had made the assumption that Claire would be the first to reach the bridge, so when he heard the footsteps above he had acted. He had already loosened all the other wooden supports and now the safety of the whole bridge had been concentrated in this one support that he had just attacked.

The bridge began to totter and then collapse. There was no time for those on the bridge to abandon it. The three on the bridge tried to hang on to the railings at the side of the bridge as it shook, but failed, and when the whole bridge fell into the river they also landed in the waters with screams of fear. It was over in a few seconds. Claire got up and ran over to the river bank and looked down at the raging waters to see if she could rescue them, but found no sign of the four youths. They had been swept away down the river, so she saw nothing of them. Four lives brought to an end all because of pride, which provoked their ire, which led them to try and murder Claire. "They could not live with the fact that a young girl had stood up to them," said Claire to a raven, sitting on what was left of the bridge. "They had to do something about it and that was to murder me and make it look like I had fallen into the river." Claire thanked God that their plan to murder her had gone awry. She then went home, not by her usual route, but by the road and that would now be her route to and from school.

Two days on and it was reported that four bodies

had been found in a calmer region of the river several miles away from the collapsed bridge and also a jeep belonging to the oldest brother had been abandoned in the vicinity of the said bridge. Later that day the names of the deceased were announced.

CHAPTER 18

Another Day Another Gang.

The King is dead, long live the King. The protection racket gang were no more, but another gang was now ready to take its place. Even before the school day had started there were three large boys, strutting about the playground telling everyone that things would resume as usual. They were now in charge and knew all about the trouble Claire had caused for the last gang. Claire had to be made an example of and they chose the morning interval to do so.

When the interval arrived, Ron and Florence were still ignoring Claire, afraid to associate with her in case this new gang would pick on them. It is not unusual that when a person stands up to a bully, the bully will not only go after that person, but the bully will also go after that person's friends. About half way through the interval, when the teacher supervising the playground was a good distance away, the gang approached Claire. "I shan't be paying you," said Claire in a loud voice. "Just go away." All those standing close by had heard Claire. Her defiance would have to be quenched, as a warning to all watching. The leader stepped forward to slap her face, but as he raised his arm to slap her a second later he found himself lying on the ground looking up at the young girl.

"I slipped", he yelled. "You're lucky I did. Have a safe journey home," he said softly to Claire, in the most threatening voice he could muster, and left with his two friends.

That very day they did have an attempt to get Claire, but she was too quick for them and it failed, so they did their homework on Claire, and found out where she stayed and what she liked to do after school, by taking turns to spy on her. They tried again to get hold of her, but again that failed. They were now furious, annoyed and very angry, so they decided to have a third attempt. Their failures had made them more and more angry and they seemed to be losing their minds.

They all came from the same district in the town, a district that was almost a no go area for the police. Almost every family there had what could be called a dangerous dog. It was there the gang met, full of boiling rage to plan the demise of Claire.

They tried again about a week later on Saturday morning. That very morning, the gang of three were to be found in the wood close to where Claire stayed. They were not alone, for each of them had brought a dog with them that they had borrowed and paid a lot of money to hire for the morning. The dogs had not been fed for a day.

CHAPTER 19

The Big Mistake

That same morning, after doing her chores, Claire went alone for a walk in the wood, as she had done a week ago, to learn more about the flora and fauna of the wood. It was when she was deep in the wood she heard the barking of dogs. "Someone is chasing a rabbit, she said. "I hope the rabbit gets away." She was sadly mistaken. It was the sound of three borrowed dogs that each member the gang had paid for. This was followed by the cry of kill, kill, kill as the three dogs were released to do their job.

They had been trained to kill by their owners, and the gang knew that when they borrowed them. Claire ran as fast as she could down a small path in the wood pursued by the dogs, while praying all the way. When she spotted what she was looking for, she leapt up into the air, grabbed hold of a branch of a tree and pulled herself up onto the tree. She let out a horrifying scream as if she had been mutilated and killed by the dogs.

It was then she heard a cheer. "It's over," cried their leader, "so let's get out of here and collect the dogs." He put his lips to a dog whistle and blew, not knowing he had just sentenced himself and his two companions to an awful death. Claire, with her remarkable hearing, heard the whistle calling the dogs back to the gang. The dogs had not been fed for a day, and they had never been together in a pack, so they knew nothing of the three gangsters who had taken them into the wood. They had been trained to kill and were now getting confused by the recall of the dog whistle for they had not yet carried out a killing. When they returned to the gang, the three gang members were grinning from ear to ear for a job well done. They soon had the grin wiped off their faces, when as soon as the dogs spotted them they ran towards the three, sprang up on them knocking them to the forest floor. The dogs had carried out the order to kill as they had been trained to do. Three youths lay dead. Claire heard their screams and sighed.

As soon as it was safe, and that was after hearing not a sound from the dogs, Claire left her tree and went looking for the carnage and it was a carnage indeed.

It was then she heard three rifle shots. "Someone has shot the dogs," she said out loud. "Probably a farmer." It was a shepherd doing his rounds and finding he was about to be set upon by three dogs. Claire then went to the place in the wood where she first heard the dogs bark. It was there, behind the bushes she found the gang members on the ground, with every bit of exposed flesh devoured. "It might be very unlikely that they will ever be found," said Claire, and departed. When she left the wood at the same place she had entered, she looked down at the fields, and spotted a young man in a farm buggy with a small trailer attached. He suddenly stopped, picked up one dead attack dog lying in the grass, and threw it into the back of the trailer. Before driving off he did this another two times. There and then Claire knelt down and thanked God for her deliverance. She then went back home, fed Hoppity Hop and Big Hen, then took her two dogs for their morning walk.

CHAPTER 20
The Piglet

One day as Claire was heading down the hill on her road to school, she heard and observed some rustling of the leaves at the foot of a very tall tree. She left the road and went over to the tree and there, almost hidden by the fallen leaves, she found a piglet scratching among the leaves on the ground. She picked it up and headed off to find Sandy. She had never been to Sandy's farm house, but she knew where it was situated, as Sandy had pointed it out to her.

When Claire arrived at the farm she noticed a young lady about to get into a car. Still holding the piglet in her arms, Claire approached the young lady. "Excuse me," she said, as the young lady turned round. "I was wondering if Sandy is about?" The young lady looked at Claire and then fixed her eyes on the piglet.

"Is that yours?" she asked Claire.

"No. I found it and was just wondering if Sandy could look after it until I returned from school, when we could then work out what to do?" said Claire.

"I'm Sandy's sister, Ethel. Just leave the piglet with me. It will be quite safe, and when you get to school you can tell Sandy all about it and discuss what to do. Sandy can't take a day off school just to look after your stray piglet. You are just being rather silly. What made you think he could?" she snapped. Claire did not know what to say, but just stared at her with her big round eyes, which made Ethel wish she had not spoken so harshly to the young girl. "By the way, what's your name?"

"I'm Claire, and it's nice to meet you, Ethel. Sandy talks a lot about you, saying you wanted to be a doctor, and he wanted to be a doctor too."

"I have not given up my struggle to be a doctor. I have all the qualifications needed to enter the course to be a doctor, but they only pick a few. I'm now on a course to be a nurse, and when I am a nurse I shall keep applying to be a doctor."

It was then a young man appeared from a building at the other side of the yard, and came over to see what was going on. "This is my brother Neven and this is Claire," explained Ethel.

"Nice to meet you, Neven," said Claire. Neven with a hand movement acknowledged the presence of Claire. The moment that Claire set eyes on Neven, she recognised him as the farmer who had shot dead the three attack dogs. Claire said nothing but kept it to herself.

"Where did you find that piglet?" Neven asked. Claire told him. "Why did you bring it here?"

"I was hoping Sandy could look after it for me,"

answered Claire, and sighed hoping to convey to Neven that she had been unsuccessful. Neven was now looking down upon a helpless young girl standing there holding a piglet in her arms which she had rescued at the roadside.

For a moment Neven forgot about the presence of his sister. Don't you worry, Claire," he cried, "Sandy's in the hen house right now. Let's go and see him." He started to go.

"What! What did you just say, Neven?" cried Ethel.

"Oops," groaned Neven, as he covered his mouth with his hand, but he was just too late. The cat was out of the bag.

"So Sandy does not go to school," asked Ethel.

"No, he doesn't, and I don't blame him," said Neven. "Why should he? Look at all the studying you did Ethel and all the good grades you got, and that lot turned your application down to study to be a doctor. It is better he works on the farm with Dad and us. If we send Sandy to school once or twice a month they will think he attends school. They don't care. If they ever send a truant officer, they will find Sandy in bed faking it. "

"I'll drag him to school if necessary," cried Ethel, "and make sure he stays there for the rest of the school day."

"I don't think you should do that," said Neven. "The whole family thinks there is no chance of him ever being allowed to be a doctor, even if he gains the best grades in the country."

"I don't agree." An argument between brother and sister broke out.

"Excuse me", spluttered out Claire, in such a voice that they just had to stop arguing and turn their attention to Claire.

"You be quiet," shrieked Ethel.

"What's it got to do with you," roared Neven.

"I too am going to do my best to be a doctor, and I shan't give up, just like you Ethel didn't give up. Importunity will be rewarded. Let me persuade Sandy to go to school. Give me a week and if I fail then you can work out what to do. Well?

"Give her a week," said Neven, having now felt guilty shouting at Claire.

"I agree," said Ethel, "but.."

"No ifs, ands, or buts, " said Claire, who seemed to be the one now in control. "We are all now going to the hen house together," and so off they went.

"Sandy I need your help," called out Claire when she looked inside the chicken coop. He looked up and saw Claire holding the piglet and smiled, but the smile vanished when he saw Ethel standing next to Claire, with a frown on her face. He agreed to look after the piglet, and Claire agreed to meet him again after school. It was then Ethel spoke.

"I shall run *both* of you to school, so you are not late and miss your class. It's on my way to the Nursing college," said Ethel, all the time with her eyes fixed on Sandy, with that same frown once again on her face.

"Thank you," said Claire, and off they went

leaving Neven not looking at all happy. Well, it did not take a week for Claire to persuade Sandy to return to school, in fact it just took a couple of days.

The same day, Claire returned after school with Sandy, to the farm so she could see how the piglet was getting on, and to speak to Ethel. Unfortunately Ethyl was not there so both Claire and Sandy went to see Neven. Neven promised to make sure that Ethel would drive Sandy to the school, so that he would have more time to do his morning chores. Before leaving, Claire found Neven and thanked him for his help. It was then Claire asked the big question. "By the way, Neven, where did you bury the three dogs?" She did not wait for an answer, but from then on Neven made sure his brother attended school every day.

CHAPTER 21

The Sunday School

Now Claire's mother had been making enquiries about the local churches and had not yet decided which one they should attend. Claire had been invited by Gwen to attend the Sunday school at her local church, so Claire accepted the invitation, and turned up early one Sunday afternoon before it was due to start. So far no one had appeared, but soon a car with a young man and woman arrived and opened up the church. Then the children came and queued up outside the church. Claire stood a short distance away and watched, and only went over to the queue when Gwen joined the queue. Just before the doors were to be opened a small group of tough-looking children, some wearing hoods arrived. There were three of them and they were there to cause trouble. They shouted obscenities at the children and tried to make fun of them. They truly were bullies, nasty people. At last the doors opened and the children entered the church.

There were about thirty children. The class was run by Miss Rankine and a Mr Lang, both being university students. As the role was called Claire noted their names, and wondered just how many were there to learn and how many to cause trouble. Gwen introduced Claire to the meeting. There were three other new children, two boys and a girl. Claire sensed trouble.

Hymn books were given out and Miss Rankine sat at the piano ready to play. The music and singing started and so did trouble. The two new boys ripped up their hymn book and threw the pieces at Mr Lang, who started to admonish the pair of them at which point the new girl got to her feet and accused Mr Lang of being a bully, and a snob only picking on poor children. She got out of her seat and rushed at Mr Lang with fist flying. Claire could see what she was up to. She wanted Mr Lang to try and stop her hitting him, and then accuse him of assault, as she made herself fall to the floor. Claire was out of her seat in a flash, and before the new girl could reach Mr Lang, Claire was there to stand in her way. Her two friends then got out of their seats and ran at Claire to push and head butt her out of the way. They did try, but unfortunately for them, there was nothing to push against except air for Claire was just too quick for them and the two boys went crashing to the floor. Miss Rankine opened the door and told them to get up off the floor and leave. One of the boys was mumbling and cursing. "Next time they want us to do this, it will cost them a lot more," he said to the others, without mumbling. "You can keep your lousy

Sunday School. We'll not be back here again for that amount." Miss Rankine accompanied them to the door along with Claire so they could not accuse her of anything when they were alone in the corridor.

Soon the lesson restarted and Bible stories were told and the gospel explained. It was like a gospel service for children where what happened on the cross was explained in ways the children could understand. Claire was very impressed and was glad Gwen had invited her. The closing children's hymn was sung and the children started to leave. The two teachers thanked Claire for her help and hoped she would be back next week. Claire suggested they should get the church to pray about how to increase the security at the Sunday School. This had been the worst incident of disruption ever at the Sunday School and thanks to Claire's intervention it had not turned into serious violence. The two teachers and Claire herself, believed that it was God who had sent her there that very day.

When Claire returned home she told her mother how the church had not used any worldly gimmicks to preach the gospel to the children, so they both attended the church next Sunday and chose that church for their family worship. Claire was also glad to hear that the church had increased the security at the Sunday School. It would now be made clear that any new children who arrived would be interviewed as to why they wanted to attend.

CHAPTER 22

A Cry for Help

One day as Claire was heading for the canteen she felt a tap on her shoulder, so she stopped and turned round. It was a girl doing her best to attract Claire's attention. "Can I help you in any way?" Claire asked the girl sympathetically, for she could see that the girl was in some sort of trouble.

"You're Claire, aren't you?" asked the girl, who was out of breath having been running to catch up with Claire before she entered the canteen.

"Yes, I'm Claire." The girl gave a big sigh of relief, but she did not say what her name was. Claire could see was worried about something. "Let's go over to a quiet part of the playground where we can talk in private," suggested Claire.

They found a quiet spot, and the girl poured her heart out to Claire. She told her that her little sister went to a nearby primary school, and that it was her job to accompany her to and from school, for their mother did not leave her work until five o'clock.

The trouble was they were being bullied by a group of girls from the same school that Claire and the girl attended. With careful questioning Claire managed to find out a little bit more about the girl and work out from that the reason for the bullying. The girl was clever, she spoke nicely and dressed modestly. "They call me all sorts of hateful names," she told Claire, "but when they start on my sister, who is only seven, then I just had to do something about it. The talk in the school is that you help people, Claire, so I was ….." It was at this moment that Claire cut in.

"Of course I'll help you," she said quickly, for she did not want the girl to have to beg her for help."

"Thank you, Claire," said the girl, as joy filled her heart, and the worried look disappeared from her brow.

"By the way, my name is Abigail and my sister is Ruth."

"These are nice names," said Claire.

"Now both the secondary school and the primary school start at the same time, but the primary school finishes earlier," explained Abigail. "However, thankfully there is an after school homework club where I can pick up Ruth." Claire reckoned that the situation needed her immediate attention and arranged to meet Abigail and Ruth after the end of the school day outside the primary school gate, and told Abigail she may be just a few minutes late.

At the end of the school day Claire went to a deserted corner of the playground where she removed a wig and a pair of spectacles from her backpack, quickly changed her appearance and then set off to the primary school to meet Abigail and Ruth.

Abigail had already arrived and was standing at the school gate with her little sister, looking anxiously around, wondering if Claire was coming or not. A girl approached them and said hello. Abigail nodded. "Are you waiting for someone?" asked the girl. Now Abigail was growing rather suspicious about this girl, for she had never seen her before and did not recognise her voice at all. "You're waiting on Claire, aren't you?" asked the girl. Abigail said not a word and the girl burst out laughing. "It is I, Claire, in disguise," whispered Claire. "I am glad you did not recognise me, because that means the disguise worked. Abigail just stood and stared, then suddenly it dawned on her that it really was Claire.

"It really is you, Claire!" she exclaimed, then burst out laughing. All this time Ruth was wondering what was going on.

"I'm a friend of your big sister," she told the little girl, and smiled. "Let's head for home now," suggested Claire, and they set out on what would become a very memorable journey.

On their road home Claire asked Abigail to video any confrontations that may occur on a smartphone that Claire handed to her, and Abigail agreed to the request. It did not take long before the bullies arrived, a boy and a girl, several years older than Claire. They regarded themselves as rebels, and they cared nothing about what others would say about them. Someone in a wheelchair was fair game to them, as were the old and forgotten. As for Abigail and Ruth, they were just fodder for their hatred. They especially hated anyone wearing a school uniform, and today they felt this was their lucky day for there was now an extra girl, three all in school uniforms, ready to be bullied. These bullies were truly sick individuals.

CHAPTER 23

The Bullying

As they were heading up a hill with houses on both sides, the two bullies started on Claire, shouting horrible things using vile language. Claire left her group and went over to the youth and stood in front of him blocking his progress up the hill. "Get out of my way," he yelled at Claire, thinking the louder he yelled the quicker she would obey, but not this time. Again he yelled at Claire with the same message, and then once more, this time with his face turning red with rage. This had never happened to him before, and for a moment he just stared at her. Claire stared back. He kept his eyes on her for a few seconds more before he flinched.

"I'll get out of your way if you just go home without shouting nasty things at me and my friends. Just be a good big boy and go home with your friend." The youth just could not believe that this young girl had stood up to him making him almost lose his mind. He lunged at her, but Claire simply stepped aside, causing him to land face down in the gutter. With one foot on his back, pressing down whenever he tried to get up. Claire got hold of his arms and tied his hands together with a length of string from her pocket. She had come prepared. She then got hold of his belt and lifted him onto the pavement and left him there, while she made her way over to his companion in bullying. Claire looked her in the eye, for that was all that was needed to make her flee up the road as if a wild dog was pursuing her.

It was then the front door of a nearby house opened and an elderly woman came out into her garden, opened her garden gate, and approached the three girls. "Well done, girls!" she called out. "That pair of bullies deserve all they got. They have been picking on children coming and going to school for far too long. Do come into the kitchen and have a cup of tea and a bite to eat." Claire looked at her two friends, but really at Abigail, who gave a little nod of acceptance." Claire took the elderly woman aside out of the hearing of the bully. "We would love to," said Claire. "We just don't want the bully to know where you stay and start annoying you. If you go back into your house we will meet you in a few minutes." Claire got him to his feet and marched him to the top of the hill. She warned him never to call people she knew names, or anyone else also. She then went over to Abigail and brought back her phone and held it right in his face. "This is *my* phone," she told him, and if you want it you will have *me* to deal with. If you do any more bullying then what just happened will be on social media for all the world to see."

Claire, without being noticed, slipped the phone into Abigail's hand. She got the message. "Bullying girls much younger than yourself is just not on. Do you know what will happen to you when that is shown?" He said not a word, but Claire could hear him grinding his teeth. She took that as an imminent warning signal.

Claire then cut the string which had bound his hands together behind his back. He was free once more, but still he desperately wanted revenge. Claire now began to walk down the hill for Abigail and Ruth had moved further away. The bully's face was turning red, his eyes were almost popping out their sockets and foam from his mouth was dribbling down his chin. Abigail was secretly recording it all on the smartphone. "I'll flatten her and smash that phone," he said to himself, with his eyes concentrated on Claire's back "That will teach her," he muttered spitefully.

He just could not resist it. He started to run towards Claire with the intention of pushing her to the ground and then stamping on her head. However, Claire heard the patter of his advancing feet and just at the right moment turned and faced him. She stood in his way with her hands on her hip watching him closely as he got closer and closer. Just as he was an arm's length from Claire, she dived to the side so he did his best to follow in her direction in the hope of grabbing hold of her. Alone he hit the tarmac on his side and rolled a couple of turns down the hill. Once again Claire bound his wrists behind his back, marched him to the top of the hill, where just a short distance away stood the girl he had been with. "You two go home now," Claire ordered them, "and if you cause any more trouble, then I shall download on social media from *my* phone, what just happened," said Claire, in a tone of voice that showed she really meant it. "I shall show a little girl humiliating you, and your girlfriend."

"I'm not his girlfriend," snapped the girl, who was watching and listening to what was going on. "I don't ever want anything to do with him again," she cried, and turned her back on him, then off she ran heading for home, while the bully boy slunk away to his own home. "Job done," said Claire, and thanked God for his protection. She then kept her appointment to have a cup of tea in the kitchen with the lady, along with her new friends Abigail and Ruth.

CHAPTER 24

The Flower Shop

It wasn't just a cup of tea they had in the kitchen, but more like an afternoon tea. They found out the lady was a certain Mrs Hay who had a flower shop in the town, which was now run and owned by her daughter. The shop also sold greeting cards and flower vases. "You girls are the first people I have ever seen dealing with these bullies," said Mrs Hay, with much gratitude in her voice. "I'm afraid the residents here, including myself and my friend Miss Willow, are just too frightened to do anything, because we are afraid of getting our windows smashed in, or pushed around in the street.

Claire then asked about the flower shop. She had heard that there was a lot of shoplifting in the town, and she wanted to know if anything like that happened in the flower shop, besides other things. "I love flowers," said Claire, "but this house where we stay in the servants' quarters, just won't have any flowers in the house. May I visit your flower shop one Saturday afternoon just after the painting club has closed. In the morning I go to the painting class, and would love to take some photos of the flowers so I could use them to help me paint?"

"I'm afraid that is not a very good time to visit the shop, Claire," said Mrs Hay, and said no more. She was afraid if she told Claire what really went on she just might want to do something about it, and that would risk the girl being badly beaten up.

"I understand," said Claire, looking rather disappointed. Unaware, Mrs Hay did not know what she had just said was like a red flag to a bull to Claire.

"What is it you paint, Claire?" asked Abigail.

"Right now I am doing paintings of birds. I take photos of them and then use the photos to help me paint them accurately."

"I would love to see some of your work, now you know where I live," said Mrs Hay. "I'm a member of the Local Bird Preservation group and so is my near neighbour Miss Willow." She then went on to chat with Abigail and Ruth. When it was time to leave the three girls felt that they had made a new friend. Claire then made sure that Abigail and Ruth got home safely, and headed off for home. As she did so she made plans for Saturday afternoon.

Now when Saturday came along and the Art Club had ended, Claire entered an empty room where she disguised herself before leaving the building. She was soon to be found at a bus stop on the street which gave Claire a good view of the shop. There she patiently watched who went in and out of the shop. She had a good idea of who it was she was waiting for, and when she spotted him she knew she was right. Down the street came a rough looking, swaggering grown up thug with a stupid grin on his big round face, topped with a stupid looking hairstyle. He entered the shop by pulling down the handle and kicking open the door. "He is probably there to collect flowers for his girlfriend for the weekend," Claire said to herself, as she followed him into the shop. Apart from the shop owner behind the counter they were the only two in the shop.

"Let's see what you have got this week, you old bag," he growled at the shopkeeper, "and don't think of phoning the police this time, or I shall smash every vase in the shop." You know they won't come anyway for flowers." He collected a bunch of flowers along with a few cards and went to leave without paying, but unfortunately for him there stood a little boy with his arms folded.

"Excuse me, you haven't paid for the flowers and cards mister," he said, while showing no fear to the thug. "You can't leave without paying, you know." The thug looked down at Claire, for who else could it be other than Claire, with his mouth wide open in unbelief. He went to punch Claire, but she saw his approaching fist aimed at her in slow motion, and moved to the side. His fist instead of striking Claire in the stomach hit the reinforced glass panel of the door causing the thug to yell out in pain, for he had just broken several bones in his right hand. He dropped the flowers from his other hand and let out a torrent of abuse at Claire. He then ran over to the shelf of vases so he could hurl them at Claire, and hopefully land at least one on her face. He never reached the shelf for Claire stuck out her foot, tripping him up and landing him flat on his face with an agonising scream, as he tried to stop his fall by stretching out his damaged hand. He just lay there, for if he moved the pain in his hand became unbearable.

Claire lifted him up by the back of his belt as if she was just carrying a suitcase. When the coast was clear she crossed over to the other side of the road then headed for the nearby empty bus shelter getting several strange looks on the way. Claire now laid the thug face down on the metal seat with his mangled hand hanging down at his side. She left the shelter and headed for home with passers by wondering what on earth was going on.

CHAPTER 25

Dogs in the Park

Early one Saturday morning, Claire decided to explore the local park. She did not know if dogs were allowed in the park so she left them at home. When she entered the park through the impressive gates all she spotted was an elderly lady walking her little dog, and a young man a further distance away with a much larger dog.

Claire was enjoying herself identifying the different types of trees, birds and flowers when the incident occurred. "Go get her," cried the cruel, vicious voice of a youth which rent the air, scattering a host of sparrows which Claire had been feeding. Claire looked up and spotted a youth in the process of releasing a large dog from its lead while pointing to the elderly lady and her little dog. The youth started to yell with delight to encourage his dog as it drew closer and closer to the lady, who had now become aware of the danger, and was now kneeling down to pick up her dog and flee. The thug was not at all interested in the elderly lady, for he only wanted to see the little dog being ripped apart, but if the lady got hurt in any way, well that was not going to bother him at all.

However, things did not work out the way he had imagined, for Claire the instant she saw what was happening, had sprinted across to the aid of the lady. She positioned herself in front of the lady and waited for the dog to arrive. The dog was confused. A second ago it had seen a small dog in the arms of a lady, but now it was a young girl. Nevertheless, it kept going and was now going to attack Claire, who now ran toward the bounding dog which confused it even more. It leapt at Claire with its foaming mouth and its jaws wide open ready to grasp Claire by the throat. The thug watching and filming all this was filled with ecstasy and let out a cry of delight. Claire, with her special gifts, when she was in danger would see things in slow motion and that is exactly what happened. She simply stepped aside when the dog leapt up to sink its teeth into Claire's throat. Claire caught hold of its tail, held onto it for just a second, turned round, placed it on the ground and off it went back to whence it came.

The dog, still thinking that it was on its original mission, was now quite confused, and thought that the youth was now its target. On reaching the youth it leapt up into the air, grabbed his throat with its massive teeth and closed its jaw. All was quiet as the thug fell to the ground. Claire ran to help the young man, but when she drew near to him, she stopped running, and now walked gingerly towards him all the time watching the dog. Claire did not get too close for with her remarkable eyesight she could see the youth was dead.

It was then Claire spotted the phone he had been using lying close to him. She just knew she had to get hold of it, for she was sure that she would be identified as the girl who had stopped the dog attacking the elderly lady and sending the dog back to where it came from. She would be held responsible for the death of the youth and would have a target on her back. The dead youth's family and friends might seek revenge and try to kill her.

Claire stood and watched in horror as the dog made a meal of the corpse. "The dog had obviously not been fed for several days, so it would become as vicious as possible. What kind of person would do that?" Claire asked herself, while still keeping her eyes fixed on the attack dog. "If I chase it, it will most likely attack me, or the elderly lady or someone else, but I *must* get that phone."

Claire was now coming to the view that the youth was surely just a thug, probably a friend of the missing gang that had tried to kill her with their dogs just a few days before. "I think today that this thug was actually trying to kill that elderly lady and not after the little dog. I recall him shouting 'go get her' as he released the dog, but I don't think he knew whether the dog was male or female. No, he was trying to kill the old lady. He must have been training it to kill. He has certainly trained it well. If his friends find his phone they will try and kill me."

Claire was hesitating no more. Very slowly she approached the phone and hence the dog, which was watching every small step she took. When she came in reach of the phone she gingerly bent down and picked it up. She knew that at any moment the dog could leap up and go for her throat, so she slipped the phone into her pocket leaving both hands free if the dog attacked. Only then she slowly rose to her feet and took small steps backwards away from the dog. Soon she was taking even larger steps with her eyes on the dog all the time. When she judged it to be safe she started walking normally whilst listening carefully and constantly turning her head to see what the dog was up to.

As she walked back, Claire got out one of her phones from her backpack and phoned the police and told them in the voice of a very old man that a dog in the park was causing chaos and had just killed a youth. She was delighted to see that the elderly lady was still there, for she had been watching from behind a tree what had been going on.

Claire approached the lady to see if she needed help, but before she could ask, the lady spoke. "Are you quite alright?" she asked "I saw you phoning. Was it the police?"

"Yes it was, but don't tell anyone. It could put my life in danger."

"I understand," said the lady. "Now are you really sure you are all right?" she asked once more, as she stared into Claire's eyes, but before Claire could answer she spoke again. "I think you better come home with me. No one your age should ever have to experience such things as you have just witnessed. I am a retired nurse and I prescribe that you come home with me and have breakfast and a cup of tea to calm your nerves. Come along now," and so saying she headed for home with her little dog trotting along at one side of her and Claire on the other. As they walked they heard the sirens of police cars and an ambulance. Shortly later on there was the sound of rifle fire.

CHAPTER 26

An Old Acquaintance

When they came to the street where the elderly lady lived, Claire immediately recognised it as the street where her friend Mrs Hay stayed. "I have been here before," said Claire. "You don't happen to know my friend Mrs Hay the florist, do you?" The lady suddenly stopped, so Claire also stopped along with the dog. The lady turned and looked at Claire. "You're Claire!" she exclaimed.

"Yes, I'm Claire," said Claire, and smiled. It had dawned on Claire that the lady at her side must be Miss Willow who Mrs Hay had spoken off.

"So you must be her good friend Miss Willow?" asked Claire.

"Yes!" she exclaimed. "I'm Miss Willow, so you, Claire, must be the friend of Abigail and Ruth?"

"Yes," said Claire, and both just had to smile.

"I must go now and tell Mrs Hay that we have met. You don't mind if I do?" asked Miss Willow.

"Of course not," answered Claire. "I too would like to meet her."

"Look who I have found," cried Miss Willow when Mrs Hay opened the door. She invited them into the kitchen, along with Miss Willow and her dog Dusty, to share breakfast with her.

Claire had to phone her mother to tell her what had happened and obtain permission to join the two elderly ladies. Well she did and the three of them were soon seated around the kitchen table each ready to start on a plate of hot porridge with milk and cream.

Claire was about to suggest that grace be said, but was beaten to it, when Mrs Hay bowed her head and said a very nice prayer of thanks. As they ate Mrs Hay related to her neighbour the awful thing that had just happened in the park. She ended her gripping narrative by telling her friend what had happened to the youth. "The dog jumped on the boy and dug its teeth into his throat, causing him to fall down on his back. It was horrible. There was blood everywhere and the dog was…. Oh! I can't go on." Miss Willow placed her two elbows on the table and sank her head into her hands. Mrs Hay rose from her seat and placed a comforting arm around her friend. "If only I had let the dog chase Dusty that poor boy would still be alive."

"It's not your fault," said Claire, sympathetically, but firmly. "When I appeared it ran back to its master. The youth should have kept the dog on its lead." So saying she folded her arms with a defiant look, daring any of the ladies to contradict her. She just was not going to watch a kind old lady blaming herself for what had happened.

"Was it his dog?" asked Miss Willow.

"Yes it was," said Claire. "I saw them together when I entered the park. He set his dog on you and Dusty. I think we should thank God for our deliverance." Claire did not need to ask Miss Willow to pray. She bowed her head, closed her eyes and thanked God.

Claire, wanting to think of something to take Mrs Willow's mind away from the horrific scene of the death of the youth, noticed a violin case in the corner of the room. "Do you play the violin, Mrs Hay?" asked Claire, as she cast a glance towards the violin case.

"Yes I do, and my friend Miss Willow plays the cello. Isn't that correct Miss Willow?"

"Oh, yes it is and we play in a local musical quartet in care homes and in halls."

"I would love to hear you play one day," said Claire.

"Are you interested in music, Claire?" asked Mrs Hay, for both the ladies could see she was genuinely interested.

"Very much," replied Claire. "I play the piano and I like to sing. I have done both in public."

"We have a pianist in our quartet, Claire, but we are always looking for singers," said Mrs Willow

"I would love to sing for you," said Claire.

"Could you sing something for us now?" asked Mrs Hay.

"If I could help somebody, would that do?" enquired Claire.

"We don't have any music for that hymn," said

Mrs Hay, "but there is a piano in the living room if you are interested." For Claire it was good news, so they all went to the living room. Claire's eyes sparkled when she saw the piano. "It was my husband's piano, but I'm afraid I have never learned to play," explained Mrs Hay. "He was a very good player," she added, as she thought back to happier times before she became a widow. "It has not been played since his death."

Miss Willow began to feel uneasy, for she felt that her friend, unwittingly, was putting undeserved pressure on Claire. "Just do your best, Claire," she said, "for that is all we ask."

Mrs Hay now realised she had made a blunder. She went up to Claire sitting at the piano and placed a comforting hand on her shoulder. "We are not here to criticise," was all she said.

"I shall do my best to keep to the high standard of play this piano has been used to," said Claire. She composed herself, and then started to play the introduction. Just at the right moment she started to sing and oh how she sang. The room had never before been filled with such a beautiful rendering of a song. The two ladies watching and listening were filled with awe and wonder at her singing and paid little attention to her piano skills. When Claire had finished she looked over at them and smiled. They were lost for words. "I'm going home now to collect my two dogs. Then we all shall go for a walk, a walk of defiance, to let the world know that we will not be intimidated by a wayward youth."

That night, as Claire sat in her chair charging herself, she thought about these dangerous dogs that she had been encountering recently. It seemed to her that the latest fad was to own a dangerous dog and record videos of their dog attacking other dogs, and perhaps people. She had heard it said that there were no dangerous dogs, but just bad owners. "Certainly the owner of the dog that had just attacked Miss Willow was a very bad one," said Claire, as she sat in her chair while going over the events of the day in her mind.

CHAPTER 27
The Self-portrait

Claire enjoyed her time in the art class. She liked the teacher, a Mr Clark, who always encouraged his pupils and never had a disparaging word about their work. Before starting on a picture he would always tell the children to remember to fill the frame. Well, today the children had to paint a self-portrait. The pupils had been asked, if possible, to bring in a printed photo of themselves, and where that was not possible they would do it all for themselves on the classroom equipment. They had to begin with a pencil drawing, and when that was finished they could start the painting. To encourage them he told the class he would hang all the paintings in the corridor just for a week. It was then a boy raised his hand to ask a question. "Yes, what is it, Clifton?" asked Mr Clark.

"Sir, why not leave the best painting in the corridor for a month?" Now Mr Clark regarded Clifton as his best student and he knew that Clifton's self-portrait would probably turn out to be the best, but there was a problem. The boy was full of pride and was rather arrogant, so his suggestion was rejected. Mr Clark just wanted him to be a little less proud, and maybe show a humble attitude now and again. It turned out that Mr Clark's hope was all in vain.

It was a double period and soon most of them had started to paint. Mr Clark urged them all to make a good job of it and not to rush. He then went round the classroom helping and encouraging the class. When he came to appraise Claire's work he was really impressed. "Amazing!" he gasped, as he fixed his eyes on her self-portrait. "That is the best self-portrait I have ever seen as a teacher. You have captured your personality on paint with such skill. Well done!" Just a second after having said these words he realised he had gone too far. It would cause others to be jealous of Claire. Mr Clark wished he had not spoken like that, but he could not help it, for he had been so amazed by Claire's work.

A few minutes later Claire went to the sink to get fresh water to clean her brush. When she returned to her place she saw what had been done to her portrait and smiled. She turned and looked at Clifton who was staring at her, with a smirk on his face daring her to do anything about it. He wanted Claire to know that he was the culprit and nothing would be done about it.

Claire knew only too well what would happen if she named Clifton as the culprit. She was a new girl in the school and she felt she would get no help from anyone in the class. As for telling Mr Clark what had just happened to her portrait, what could he do about it? "If I accuse Clifton of vandalising my work, then he will probably say that he never left his place when I was at the sink. He would then say his painting was the best in the class and accuse me of messing up my own painting, because it was inferior to his." Claire decided to take no action and just ignore what happened.

She dipped her sponge in her water jar and applied it to her portrait, wiping away the freshly applied brush strokes of black paint that had been added by Clifton. It did work, but it also removed parts of her own work, so she knew that she really would have to start over again on a new sheet of paper. She did her best to restore the painting, but just a few minutes later Mr Clark announced that it was time to pack up and to get ready to leave. They were to leave their paintings in a corner of the room ready to be hung the next time the class met. When the bell rang they filed out of the room, followed by Mr Clark, with all of them heading to the canteen.

In the canteen, as Claire was enjoying her lunch, she looked over at Clifton in the far side of the canteen and sighed. He was proud of his reputation of being the best artist in his year group and probably in the whole school, and he was adamant that he was not going to have this slip of a new girl, to outshine him. Claire did not hate him, but she did feel sorry for him, for she knew that *pride cometh before a fall*. What would happen to him? Well she would just have to wait and see.

CHAPTER 28

Art for All

Next day, Mr Clark came in well before the start of school to hang up the self-portraits in the corridor outside his class room. He started by placing the paintings on a trolley when suddenly he gave out a gasp of surprise when his eyes fell upon Claire's self-portrait "What on earth has happened to Claire's painting?" he asked himself. "It's been vandalised. Who on earth would do such a thing?" He then started to examine the painting for clues. He could see the parts of the picture that had been removed with the sponge. He soon came to the truth. "Someone has marked the painting and Claire has used a sponge to remove it, while at the same time removing her own work," said Mr Clark with a heavy sigh, but ploughed on, and was soon to be found in the corridor hanging the portraits.

When Claire's class arrived for art that same day, most of the children were delighted to see their work displayed in the corridor. None of the class noticed that Claire's portrait was missing except Clifton, and of course Claire herself. A smirk had now appeared on Clifton's face that lasted for the whole of the period, and probably for much longer. At the end of the period, it was the morning interval, so some in the class hung around to admire their painting. "Sorry about your painting, Claire," said Mr Clark. It was then he handed Claire a flyer advertising an art class, open to the pupils and the public, which would meet every Saturday morning, at nine o'clock in the school. The teacher would be Mr Clark, himself. "Do come," he said, as he locked his classroom door and then headed off for the staffroom. Claire read the flyer. The class was for painting in oils and watercolour, and also for those interested in drawing, photography and picture framing.

Well Claire did attend, and was met by Mr Clark at his classroom door. Most of the school was closed down except the Gym hall and the Art and Music wing of the school. A small fee should have been levied for younger students, but Mr Clark waived the fee in the drive for recruitment for younger artists, and paid it out of his own money. All the other people in the class looked like adults of all ages.

It was a large classroom for it had been designed not only for pupils, but for night classes and weekend classes for all. When asked what she wanted to paint, Claire chose to do an oil painting of herself sitting at a grand piano. Now it just so happened that there was a music classroom close by, the very one where Miss Bevan taught and where Gwen would practise on the grand piano. "I have a good idea," suddenly cried Mr Clark. "It just came to me. Why not go to the music room down the corridor? It's got a grand piano and you could work out what type of photo you would like. The room is not locked so the cleaners can get in. It has a secure store room, so why not?"

"I would like to," said Claire. "I will go now and come back in ten minutes, as I want to soak up the atmosphere of sitting playing the piano to a make-believe audience?"

"Do you play the piano?" asked |Mr Clark.

"Yes I do," replied Claire, and sighed. "However, I seldom get a chance to play any sort of piano nowadays, never mind a grand piano." At this point Claire looked up at Mr Clark with her large pleading eyes and sighed once again. What else could Mr Clark do, but suggest to Claire she actually went to the music room and played the piano. He felt there was no harm in that, as he knew Miss Bevan permitted certain pupils to use it.

"I'll come back later with my most excellent photographer, and she will take your photo sitting at the piano, then you can start with the oils along with the rest of the class.

CHAPTER 29
Claire the Pianist

When Claire arrived at the music room she just had to smile when she saw the grand piano. She sat down on the stool, lifted the lid and started to play. She seemed to float back in time to when she was playing in a concerto with Sir Robert Buchanan conducting, and her mother and friends there in the audience. She played and played her favourite pieces of music, losing all sense of time.

Soon it was time for Mr Clark along with Emily, one of his school pupils, to go and see if Claire was ready to have her photo taken. As he was walking down the corridor towards the music room he was stopped in his tracks when he heard the piano being played with such skill. He thought the sound was coming from a radio, but only for a second. When he arrived at the music room he opened the door, expecting to see a grown-up sitting playing the piano with Claire watching and listening. He could hardly believe his eyes when he saw it was Claire sitting at the piano in an empty room. "Is that really you, Claire?" he called out, as he stood watching.

Claire stopped playing and looked up to see Mr Clark standing at the open doorway with Emily. "Oh!" exclaimed Claire, "is it time for me to get my photo taken?"

"Yes it is," replied Mr Clark. He then introduced Clare to Emily.

"It's nice to meet you, Emily. I have seen you at school," said Claire.

"And it's nice to meet you too, Claire. Yes I am in my final year at school. I don't think I have seen you before."

"I'm new. I haven't been there long. Mr Clark is my teacher," said Claire.

"He's mine too," said Emily.

"I always get the best pupils," said Mr Clark.

Several photos were taken and printed so Claire now could start work on her canvas. She did not finish it that day, but she did finish it a fortnight later.

Now, when Mr Clark saw Claire's finished work on the easel, he stepped back to admire it and then to view it close up. "Remarkable," he whispered to Claire. It really was remarkable, for it depicted Claire sitting at the grand piano in a concert hall, with one eye on the conductor, a certain Sir Robert Buchanan, and the other on the keyboard. "Quite remarkable!" he whispered, almost to himself thinking not even Claire could hear, but he had been mistaken. Claire just looked at him and smiled. It was at that very moment that Mr Clark had a funny feeling that he just knew he had seen her somewhere before. "You had better sign your painting, Claire," he suggested, while thinking that if he saw her signature that it may jog his memory.

Mr Clark was very keen that the class would learn to frame their work, for he felt that having spent hours painting or taking photos and printing them, that their work deserved to be framed and viewed. Claire selected a fine brush, selected the colour white from her pallet, and signed her name just with the single name Claire, at the bottom right hand side of the canvas. It was executed in such a manner that if anyone wanted to find it they would have to closely scrutinise the painting. As Mr Clark watched her sign, it was then he had his moment of realisation of who Claire really was. It affected him in such a way that he took a step back to lean against the classroom wall. He then called Emily over to see Claire's work, for after all she was the one who had taken the photograph. Emily was impressed so Claire thanked her for taking such a good photo. Claire then went over to Emily's painting and Claire too was impressed and told Emily so. Claire was not just being polite for she just had to admire her work. It was a painting of a garden bird, a very good painting indeed, of a goldfinch.

Soon it was time to lock up. As the class filled out and Mr Clark stood at the door waiting to lock up, he noticed Claire chatting to Emily. "By the way, Claire," he said, could the conductor in the painting happen to be Sir Robert Buchanan?"

"Yes," replied Claire.

"And is that you playing the piano?"

"Yes, it is," said Claire modestly.

"Did that really happen or is it just an imaginary painting?"

"Well Mr Clark, if you promise not to tell anyone, and if Emily also promises, then that's me in the Royal Albert Hall playing Tchaikovsky piano concerto number one."

She looked at both with her big round eyes waiting to see if they would promise, and of course they all did.

CHAPTER 30
The Chess Club

It turned out that Claire's friend Emily was a member of the school chess club, which had been set up by a teacher who was in overall charge, but who was free to delicate the everyday running of the club to a senior pupil of the school. This school year a boy called Erwin ran the club and insisted on being addressed by the name of Mr President. His status had gone to his head and he would strut about the room while games were going on. He would tell some of the members just how pathetic they were at chess, while suggesting that they go and join some other club where they did not need to use their brain. He even went after Emily, who was actually a very accomplished player, one of the beds in the club. Erwin would challenge her and other good players, now and again, to a match which he always won. He made sure that they never forgot, for he loved to humiliate people whenever he got the chance.

One Saturday when Emily was chatting to Claire after the Art club, Emily asked Claire a question that had been on her mind now for several weeks.

"Do you play chess?" Emily asked. She knew Claire was talented in many things and she wondered if that included chess.

"Yes I do," said Claire, causing Emily to breathe a sigh of relief which she tried her best to muffle, but not enough to stop Claire hearing the expression of thankfulness.

"How can I help you?" asked Claire. Emily told Claire about the horrible attitude and manners of the so-called president of the club, so Claire agreed to attend the next meeting on Monday after she had lunch.

Well Claire did attend after lunch on Monday and was granted membership of the club after an interview with Erwin. She then had a game with Bert, a boy about her own age, which resulted in a draw. It was then Erwin came to see how Claire was doing. "By what you told me at your interview, I thought you were a much better player than that. You were playing the most useless member of the club and you could not even beat him," said Erwin, for all in the room to hear. The poor boy just raised his eyes to the ceiling and said not a word, for he was used to having to bear the brunt of Erwin's insults. Claire felt it was now time for her to stand up for herself and Bert. All those in the room had heard the insults and looked over to see how it had affected the new girl. Claire caught the eye of Emily who now wished she had not asked Claire to join the club. Claire gave her a smile as much to tell her not to worry.

"I think Bert is a very good chess player," said Claire, looking straight at Erwin as she rose to her feet to confront him. "In fact, I found him hard to beat so hence the draw, unlike people like you Erwin, who are supercilious and all bluster. I think it would be much easier to defeat you in a game of chess than Bert." Erwin was starting to grow angry, for he never had anyone in the chess club speak to him before like that. There was no way Claire would go about defeating members, for that was not her nature. On the other hand, she would not hesitate in defeating the imperious Erwin to teach him a lesson in good manners.

Erwin's face was growing redder and redder every second as he became more and more angry. "Very well, if that's what you think, then right here and now challenge you to a game of chess when the club opens thirty minutes after the start of the lunch break tomorrow. Not for a minute did he think Claire would accept his challenge.

"I accept your challenge," said Claire, in a confident tone of voice. "I'll be there after lunch, but the question is, Erwin, will you be there? He certainly did not like getting a bit of his own medicine from a little girl like Claire.

Claire was as good as her word, and appeared at the appointed time to take on her opponent. Word had spread round the school about the challenge, and those children who hated Claire were there, along with those who had come to support her. The referee would be the teacher in charge of the club.

When all was settled down the match started, just to end a few minutes later when the cry of checkmate was heard. Claire had won, and the result was verified by the referee. Erwin believed it was just a fluke and he could still easily defeat Claire. "Best out of three?" he growled, as he looked at Claire. Claire accepted the challenge. The room fell quiet once more with some of Claire's supporters wishing she had not accepted the further challenges, but they need not have worried. The game went ahead and once again Claire won, which was verified by the referee. Erwin just sat there looking at the board, then all of a sudden he sprang to his feet, scattering the board and chess pieces all over the floor. He stood up straight with shoulders back, looked around then immediately marched out the room slamming the door behind him. He never was seen again at the chess club for he was entirely the wrong type of person to run it. He was replaced by a more caring pupil, and from then on the chess club flourished.

CHAPTER 31
Trouble on the Train

Claire always kept in contact with Mrs Low and Bella, so when the two ladies invited Claire to visit them on Saturday morning she immediately accepted their invitation. They were to meet at the servants' quarters of the mansion, where they were now employed. Bella sent Claire a photo of the house which was situated close to where they all used to live and work. To get there she would have to take the train, so when Saturday arrived she waved goodbye to her mother and set off to the train station. As soon as she was out of sight Claire set about changing her appearance. From her back pack, which was not her usual one, she produced a wig and a different top and a pair of gloves. When she entered the station it would have taken an extremely observant person to identify the girl buying a return ticket, as Claire, the school girl. Well that is just what she wanted, for she was sure that she would run into some bully or other from the school, or perhaps some thug looking to cause trouble. It turned out that Claire was one hundred percent right on that account.

When the train arrived she found it to be rather busy, and had to sit beside three elderly ladies sitting in double spread seats with a small table between them. Claire sat down in the vacant seat and smiled across to the two ladies facing her. At the same time two youths, one of them carrying a boombox, sat down in two seats just across from Claire, where an elderly couple, husband and wife, were seated side by side. The one carrying the boombox, who was just across the aisle from Claire, placed it on the small table, and looked around to see if anyone in the carriage appeared to be tough enough to take him on, for he was intent on causing trouble. He made a big mistake, for Claire was watching him and his friend.

Just as the train was leaving the station he turned on his boombox with a sneer of contempt for the passengers. Everyone turned round to find out who was causing the sound of the awful, so-called music. It sounded to Claire more like a metal dustbin lid being struck every third second by a steel bar, or a dripping tap in a room. It truly was dreadful for it was meant to cause trouble.

"Excuse me," shouted the elderly man, sitting facing him, "you are upsetting myself and my wife with that loud noise. Could you please turn the volume down, or better still, just switch it off."

"Shout your mouth, you old fool," yelled the thug, doing his best to annoy the elderly gentleman even more. To make the situation even worse he positioned the boombox, so that the speaker now faced his wife.

"How dare you!" exclaimed the elderly gentleman, as he rose from his seat to move the boombox from the table. He never did get to his feet for the thug had thrust out his hand and shoved him back in his seat with undue force. It was a cruel thing to do for the old gentleman let out a scream of pain when he landed back in his seat.

"You are just a horrible bully," cried the elderly lady sitting facing Claire. "Just leave that gentleman and his wife alone."

"Just shut your face or you'll get the same treatment," yelled the thug, who seemed to revel in his bullying behaviour.

Claire, who had witnessed it all, and who felt she should have perhaps acted sooner, leapt up and pushed the thug back into his seat, with even more force that he had inflicted on the old gentleman. As the thug lay in his seat stunned, wondering what on earth had happened, Claire switched off the loud music, and laid the boombox down at the feet of the thug. She then took a few steps back, and stood just watching him, ready for his next move.

He then slowly got up, went into the aisle and stood growling at Claire, causing her to move further away from him. Claire smiled at him and placed her hands on her hip. He started to breathe very heavily, and with a yell he charged at Claire hoping to headbutt her, so she would scream with pain as she collapsed to the floor, but unfortunately for him that never happened. Claire stepped into a double spread seat that was just occupied by a father and son. It was inevitable that the thug would land face down in the aisle.

Claire thought he would have had enough, but he was having none of that. He quickly jumped up and pulled out a concealed knife from his belt. He rushed at Claire hoping to plunge the blade deep into her heart. The young girl had just humiliated him, and he was now experiencing feelings he had never felt before. He had murder on his mind, and nothing was going to stop him. He lunged at Claire with his knife in hand, but Claire saw it all in slow motion. She grabbed his hand with such force that the knife fell from his grasp and landed on the aisle. Claire took a step back, pulled him towards herself, and side stepped him so he went flying up the corridor again landing on his face. She then went up to him, put her foot on his back, tore off his top and ripped it up so she could get a strip of cloth to tie his wrists together behind his back.

Claire did the same with his feet, after removing his boots. She then picked up the knife with her gloved hand and laid it at the feet of the thug. "Leave your pal there," ordered Claire, to the thug's astonished friend, as she walked to take up her seat with the three ladies. No one said a word for they did not know just what to say, except the husband of the wife who had been disgustingly verbally abused. He thanked Claire while his wife gave the young girl a thank you smile. Claire reached out and gently squeezed her hand in order to show her admiration for the brave elderly lady.

No one quite knew what to do with the bully tied up and lying on the floor, especially his friend who was terrified that the same fate could happen to him, so for the first time in many months he just sat there and behaved as good as gold. When the announcement came over the speaker that they were nearing Claire's destination, the ticket collector appeared so Claire quietly slipped away and headed for the carriage door. When the train stopped and Claire left the station, she was actually followed by the friend of the thug, but Claire very soon ended that. "I think he was just doing it, as an excuse for deserting his friend in his time of need," said Claire. She then changed back to look like Claire once more.

As she went on her way she wondered once again if she should have acted sooner. Should she have attacked the bully before the bully laid hands on the elderly gentleman. If that had happened that would have given the bully a just cause to start the fight. "No," said Claire, "I think I chose the right way." She then thanked God for looking after her."

CHAPTER 32

Together Again

On arriving at the mansion Claire found her way barred by the large gates, and had to press the intercom. It was Bella who answered and she of course let Claire through. Claire walked swiftly to the servants' quarters where she met up with Mrs Low, who was walking as fast as she could to give Claire a huge hug of welcome. Claire ran to her and fell into her outstretched arms. Through her misty tears Claire could see Bella smiling and watching knowing just how much Mrs Low had longed to see Claire once again. They then went inside where the table was set for a snack. Mrs Low said grace thanking God for the food they were about to eat, and being together again.

"How long have you been working in this house?"asked Claire.

"We are here only for six weeks," said Mrs Low. "The lady of the house had a baby girl and we are just helping out until things settle back to normal. We often get jobs when people are looking for help for just several weeks, or a few months. Bella and I have a good reputation and are always kept busy.

"That's because Mrs Low is the best cook in the district," whispered Bella.

"Now that's not quite right, Claire. We work as a pair," said the modest Mrs Low, who had overheard the whisper.

As Claire was munching away at Mrs Low's scones, Bella had some more news to tell. "We have heard rumours that Mrs Toeser, who we used to work for, is making such a mess of her job that she and her husband will soon be replaced. Once they find a suitable family to replace her, then she and her husband will be on their way. I shall let Mrs Low tell the rest."

"We think that the newcomers would need a housekeeper soon," said Mrs Low, "and if they do, we would love to recommend your mother, if the opportunity arrives. What do you think, Claire?" asked Mrs Low, hoping she would be pleased at the news. She was not disappointed.

"That is wonderful news," said Claire. "The three of you working together again. I'm sure my mum will be delighted too, but she will have to pray about it, of course. I shall ask her to contact you when I get back." Time flew by and soon it was time to leave, for both the ladies had their duties to perform. Claire gave Mrs Low her special farewell hug, and thanked them both for the pleasant time they had spent together. Claire would have liked to visit Mrs Flower's but she had learned that she had taken Jennifer to play in an important cricket match, so Claire just headed to the station knowing that her train would soon be due. After what had happened on the train she came in, Claire reasoned that it would only be wise to disguise herself once more. She knew the district well, so she went along a dirt path, hid behind a bush and a minute later emerged as a boy. Finally she sorted out things in her backpack, and placed the backpack in a larger cloth carrier bag.

When she arrived at the station she found herself to be justified in taking such precautions, for there was the friend of the knife thug, along with what Claire presumed to be his gang, obviously looking out to inflict harm on her. Alone he had been terrified of Claire, but now along with other thugs he felt quite secure. Claire walked past them along the platform, and positioned herself so that she would board the front carriage of the train when it arrived. She was soon to be home again safe and sound.

CHAPTER 33
A New Friend

One Saturday morning on her way to the Art Club, Claire noticed an elderly lady struggling with her garden waste wheelie bin. She was trying to fit a rather thick fallen branch into the bin, but it was just a little bit too long to fit. Claire immediately noticed that the lady was the very same lady she had sat beside in the train on her visit to Mrs Low and Bella. "Can I help you?" called out Claire. The lady stopped her struggle and looked over at Claire. She looked Claire up and down to vet her, and came to the conclusion that Claire's offer of help was genuine. She was going to thank Claire for her offer of help, then tell her she could manage quite well on her own, but for some reason or other she could not explain, she actually accepted the offer of help.

"The branch just won't fit and I have lots of others to gather up and put in the bin. Come and see," called the elderly lady. Claire opened the garden gate and walked up to the lady.

"Let's see if I can make this pesky branch fit into the bin," said Claire, who removed the branch from the bin.

"It's too thick to break in two," said the lady. "There's a saw in the garden hut in the back garden, if you would like to collect it." There was a wooden fence that prevented entry into the back garden, with a gate in it which Claire could see was opened.

"You should not let strangers into your back garden for they may be dangerous," said Claire, not meaning to lecture the lady, but only because she was concerned about her safety after the incident on the train.

"You are so right, for I would not do such a thing normally, but just for a moment I had this strange feeling that I felt I knew you, and you could be trusted." At this point Claire decided to reveal who she was.

"It might be a flashback to when you were on the train along with that thug with a knife who tried to kill that little girl," suggested Claire.

"How did you know about that?" exclaimed the elderly lady, who looked so surprised.

"I knew it, because I was that very girl he tried to kill. Don't you recognise me now? I was the girl sitting facing you when the thug turned his wrath on you, because you were the only one to stand up to help the elderly couple." The elderly lady just stood there completely dumbfounded.

Claire then went into her backpack and brought out the wig and the fake glasses she had used that eventual day, and showed them to her."Well I never! " she gasped, now able to utter a few words.

"I'm Claire, by the way. I should have told you as soon as we met who I was, but I thought it best to break it gently to you."

"I think that was most wise. I might have fainted, you never know. It's a pleasure to meet you, Claire. I'm Mrs Fisher."

"And I am honoured to meet you, Mrs Fisher. The only one to stand up to the bully on the train and support the elderly couple. We best not tell anyone that we were on the train together, just in case." Mrs Fisher knew exactly what she meant. "Now let's finish gathering up all these fallen branches under the tree and put them in the bin," said Claire as she got to work.

"Thank you, Claire, " said Mrs Fisher. "I'll go and fetch the saw."

"We shan't need the saw," said Claire, as she was bending down gathering the branches. Mrs Fisher looked surprised, but was not going to argue with her. Claire had soon gathered up a bundle of branches in her arms which she dumped down at the side of the bin, and started to fill the bin with the smaller branches. Those that did not fit she snapped in two, or three and once in four pieces and into the bin they went. Mrs Fisher looked on in surprise, but not in awesome surprise, as she was getting used to being with Claire.

"I better go now," said Claire, "but I don't think I should snap this one," which she held up for Mrs Fisher to see. It was the one that Mrs Fisher was trying to fit into the bin when Claire saw her struggling with it. "It brought us together and deserves a place in the garden." Claire looked around and placed it in a prominent position next to the tree. It was then she noticed a bird table in a small secluded part of the front garden. "Oh, there's a bullfinch on your bird table," said Claire, who had exceptional sight.

"Why not stay and watch the birds for a while?" suggested Mrs Fisher. "I also have a bird table in the back garden that you must see some time."

"I would love to," said Claire, "but I have to go now to my arts class. I could come after the class which ends at twelve." It was then she remembered Emily who liked to take photographs, and to paint pictures of birds. Claire told Mrs Fisher all about Emily and she agreed Emily could come too.

CHAPTER 34
The Finished Painting

At the start of the arts class Claire told Emily all about the meeting she had with Mrs Fisher, and the invitation of Mrs Fisher which Emily accepted. "Do you mind if I also paint birds, just like you are doing? I don't want you to think that I am just copying you, for I saw a gold finch this morning at her bird table and would love to capture it on canvas."

"Not at all, Claire. I shall look forward to seeing your finished work." said Emily, flattered that Claire also wanted to paint birds after having viewed her paintings. So Claire got down to work but after about an hour she had to stop, as it was now her turn to use the picture framing equipment. Emily had already used it and had started on another bird painting, from a photograph. She was so looking forward to using her own bird photos. Now Claire had watched on the internet how picture framing was done so it did not take her long to frame her painting of herself with the orchestra and was soon back working on her painting. She had shown the framed picture to Mt Clark, who complimented her on her work. He was truly amazed that she had finished in such a short time.

"It seems whatever she sets out to do she does well. Playing the piano, painting, it makes me wonder what else she is good at. Perhaps she is just some sort of genius," he said to himself, and paused as he looked over at Claire working busily away at her painting. "I wonder?" he asked out loud. Soon it was time to close and Mr Clark, as was his habit, went round the class to see how they were all doing. He never had a disparaging word for any member and would always encourage them in their work. When he came to Emily, he was once again very impressed with her work on the new bird painting she had started, but when he came to view Claire's painting, he was truly overwhelmed at what he saw. Emily's painting was good, not just good but very good, in his judgement. Emily was the best student he had ever taught but now had to admit to himself that Emily was now his second best.

Emily's painting as he had just stated was very good, but it looked like that of a stuffed bird that could be found in a museum. As a copyist Emily was the best, but there was something lacking. Claire's painting of a bird on the other hand looked as if the bird could leave the canvas at any moment, and fly around the room. It did not have the detail contained in Emily's painting, but it felt like a real, living bird. He complimented Claire on her work, but not as much as she deserved, for he did not want to cause any jealousy between the two girls. "Perhaps I have just been teaching the class the techniques of painting, but not how to become a great artist," he asked himself, "but I reckon that's something that just can't be taught."

CHAPTER 35

The Quartet

After the art class Claire, along with Emily, went off to visit Mrs Fisher. Claire rang the bell and Mrs Fisher answered and gave both of them a warm welcome. "After you have finished watching the birds you are welcome to join me for lunch if your parents' grant permission. They obtained permission and after watching the birds and taking photos they sat down in the dining room for lunch. Before starting, Mrs Fisher asked if any of them would like to say grace, while thinking neither of them would. Claire looked over at Emily and signalled with her eyes that she thought Emily ought to say grace as she was the elder of the two. To Mrs Fisher's surprise, Emily bent her head and thanked God for the friendship and the meal that lay in front of them. While they ate they talked about the birds, and got to know more about each other. Mrs Fisher learned that they had been working on oil paintings of birds at the art class, so she invited them to view her collection of oil paintings

So after lunch they were shown through to the

sitting room where they all sat down on the corner sofa. Mrs Fisher asked to see the girls' paintings they had brought with them. Emily showed Mrs Fisher the bird painting which she had just framed. She was very impressed, for indeed it was quite exceptional. "May I see your bird painting, Claire?"asked Mrs Fisher.

"I have not yet finished my painting of the goldfinch," said Claire. "The picture I have is of me playing the piano."

"I would love to see it anyway," said Mrs Fisher. So Claire showed her the picture and Mrs Fisher was very interested and asked Claire all about it. "Is that you in the picture, Claire?" asked Mrs Fisher. Claire nodded. "That was just like me when I was your age. I was a dreamer too, thinking that one day I too could be a virtuoso pianist." She stopped speaking and gave forth a huge sigh of regret. It was at this point Emily was going to intervene and tell Mrs Fisher that her assumptions about Claire were completely wrong, but Claire caught the eye of Emily and put her index finger to her lips. Emily got the message.

"Do you still play the piano, Mrs Fisher?" asked Claire.

"Oh yes, I do. I never gave up playing and you must also never. You never know Claire, one day that could *actually* be you sitting in that painting, playing to a large audience." Once again she paused and gave Claire a sympathetic smile. She was saying all this to encourage Claire with her playing. Meanwhile, Emily looked on feeling rather embarrassed, for Mrs Fisher had just assumed that Claire was just like Mrs Fisher when she herself was young. "Nowadays I'm a member of a quartet in which I am the pianist," said Mrs Fisher, rather proudly.

"Please tell us more about the quartet, Mrs Fisher," asked Claire.

"It consists of myself on the piano, two other ladies, one playing the violin the other the cello, and a retired gentleman also playing the violin," said Mrs Fisher, delighted that Claire had taken an interest. We are all retired and live nearby. "I guess then you could almost call us a string quartet." Claire was right to think that she probably already knew the violinist and cellist.

"I think I know the two ladies you are talking about," said Claire. "We went for a walk together in the park with our dogs."

"Oh, that will be them, all right Claire. They love their dogs." Mrs Fisher was not really interested in her friends and their dog right now, for she was keen to find out more about Emily and Claire, so she continued in the original conversation. "We play in halls to women's groups and in old folks' homes. We usually finish our session by having a sing-along, but we are short of a good singer to get them started. I don't suppose," she said, while gazing hopefully at the two friends,"that any of you two have sung in public?" Now Claire had sung in public, but waited to see what Emily was going to say. "What about you, Emily?" prompted Mrs Fisher.

"I have," said Emily.

"Oh, that is good news!" cried an excited Mrs Fisher. "Would you be willing to help the quartet?" Emily agreed, but pointed out she also had a lot of studying to do, for she was hoping to be accepted as a student at the town's Art School. Mrs Fisher, so pleased at finding a volunteer in Emily, had forgotten to ask if Claire too sang in public.

"I wonder if they could call their group a quintet when Emily sings?" said Claire to herself, also pleased at the outcome.

CHAPTER 36
The Boycott

Now Claire had stood up to several different bullies at her school who were in her year group. The nastiest of the bunch was a boy called Big Ben, who took delight in terrorising as many of the pupils as possible. He hated Claire who he regarded as a danger to his authority among the children. Using his acquiescent followers, the message spread round the school that no one had to speak with Claire or have anything to do with her. There were no threats issued along with the command, for there was no need, for every one already knew the consequences of disobeying. Claire was first to learn about the threat from Gwen, and told Claire that she was going to ignore it, but Claire knew she had to deal with the silly, big, bully boy, and told Gwen just to obey the command, for she had a plan, and it could go awry if she did otherwise. Gwen reluctantly acquiesced. Claire managed to persuade her other friends to do the same, and so now the stage was set for the big show-down, which was to start at the morning interval.

When Claire arrived at the playground at the

break it was already quite busy. She at once spotted Big Ben walking around making his presence known. He was surprised to see the presence of Claire, for he thought she would be hiding in the library, scared to show her face in public, and keeping well away from him. Contrary to what he was expecting, Claire marched right up to him and looked him in the eye. "Well, hello Benjamin," said Claire, and smiled. He just glared down at her and ground his teeth. "Nice morning, isn't it Ben?" said Claire, for all around to hear, trying her best to get him to talk. "No reply?" asked Claire. "Are you scared to talk to me too? I would just ignore the threats, it's such a silly thing to have a boycott. Don't you agree?" Claire went on and on, yapping away causing the bully's temper to grow and grow until it was about to blow. Big Ben wasn't so stupid as to strike her in a crowded playground, so not being able to trust himself he left with his face as red as a beetroot, which showed to all just how angry he was. The rumour spread round the school that Big Ben had been humiliated by a young girl.

When the next school day arrived Claire was on her guard for she was expecting Ben to react to what happened the day before. She was soon proven to be right. Claire and Ben weren't always in the same class, but they were all in the same cooking class, where they learnt to cook all sorts of things. Now as the name may apply, Big Ben was a rather portly boy and he liked his food. He had been given the gift of being a very talented cook and why he wanted to be a bully was a mystery to Claire. That day Claire thought she had the answer. "Perhaps the money he extracts from the children is used to buy lots of pies and pastas. It is better than spending the money on drugs." She was partly correct.

Also in the class was Gwen, and she was to play an important part in what was to happen. That very morning, when they met Claire asked Gwen for her help. "Could you please keep an eye on Ben in the cookery class today?" asked Claire.

"Do you think he will do something bad then?" asked Gwen.

"Yes."

"How can I help?" asked Gwen, keen to be of assistance.

"When I am away from my place, at the sink or collecting something, do you think you could keep and eyes on Ben, if he goes near my place, but not only that, and here it gets dangerous, could you video what he is up to on this phone?" which Claire now held in her hand.

"Of course I shall," said Gwen, and reached out to receive the phone. They talked further on the subject before going their separate ways.

CHAPTER 37
The Cooks

The cookery course class was held before the lunch break and was a double period, so the children could produce something they could take home. It was a very popular class, as were the woodwork and metalwork classes, to be in and they all looked forward to it, unlike the gym class, but that is another story. The day was just like any other day, so when the bell rang the children lined up outside the cookery class and were let in ready to get on with their work, knowing they were allowed to take home whatever they made.

Gwen knew she had an important part to play in Claire's plan, so she kept a close eye on what Big Ben was up to. As soon as Ben spotted the opportunity for his plan to work, he acted. Claire had to go over to the sink to clean a wooden spoon that had fallen on the floor. As she made her way to the sink, she glanced over at Gwen, who signalled with her eyes that she was fully alert to the danger. Ben was now out of his place heading to where Claire worked. No one but Gwen noticed him bending down, putting something into Claire's school bag and returning to his place. Gwen had played her part well, so when Claire was returning from the sink she gave her friend a thumbs up smile.

At the end of the lesson the children placed the scones that they had backed into the containers which they had brought with them. When Claire placed her container into her school bag she found what Ben had deposited in her bag. He had made a good job of hiding his deposit, but not good enough to fool Claire.

When the lesson ended, the children were all very pleased with their work, especially Ben. Only Claire and Gwen knew the real reason why he left the class room with a big grin all over his face. As Claire and Gwen left the room together, Gwen handed Claire back her phone. Claire looked at the video which Gwen had just made and thanked her for a good job done. "I have to go now Gwen and finish my plan. Thanks again for a good job, and enjoy your lunch," said Claire. They then parted.

Just as there was always a teacher on playground duty, there was always a teacher available in their room if anyone needed help at lunch time and the intervals. All the conversations were recorded and the children knew it. There was a rota system and the names were read out, first period, every day, from the daily information sheet.

Claire walked quickly to Miss Roger's room, the teacher on the rota for that day, who just happened to be Claire's geography teacher. Claire was the first pupil to arrive, so she knocked at Miss Roger's classroom door and was told to enter. There sitting behind her desk, doing her paperwork was Miss Rogers. "How can I help you?" she asked Claire. "You know the school rules that everything we say will be recorded. Do you agree with this?" Claire agreed.

"Someone has put some things in my bag, Miss, without my permission," said Claire.

"Could you show me them, Claire?" asked Miss Rogers.

"There are four twenty pound notes along with what I think may be drugs in two small plastic bags. I don't want my fingerprints on this stuff," said Claire. Miss Rogers got out of her seat and looked into the bag.

"Very wise, this looks suspicious" said Miss Rogers. She opened one of her desk drawers and removed a small pair of tongs which she handed to Claire. Using the tongs Claire placed the bags and money into another drawer which Miss Rogers had opened. Miss Rogers locked the drawer, and placed the key in a white envelope, sealed it, signed it, and dated it along with the time of day. "I now want you to take this envelope to the school office and get whoever is in charge to place the envelope into the safe and ask them to log it in their journal. Make sure you see them log it and see it placed in the safe. If they object just tell them Miss Rogers told you what to do. I shall look into your case and contact you later," said Miss Rogers."

As Claire was leaving there was then a knock at the door. It was a small boy wanting to see Miss Rogers. Claire immediately went to the office and handed in the envelope and told the young worker what had to be done. "You can go now," said the young man, when Claire handed him the envelope. Claire just stood and watched, "Just leave," he said, raising his voice, annoyed that Claire had not yet left. "Just go," he almost yelled at the young girl.

"Miss Rogers told me to make sure her instructions were carried out," was all Claire had to say.

"Oh, Miss Rogers, yes indeed," he said, as he stared at Claire. No more was said and Claire left only when she saw the letter safely locked up in the safe. Claire could see Miss Rogers was a force to be reckoned with. Claire knew she tolerated no nonsense in her class, and it seemed she applied that to the rest in the school. Claire then left to join her friends in the canteen, after which Gwen went to her piano practice and Claire visited the playground.

CHAPTER 38
The Silly Big Boy

Now, just before the end of the lunch break there was a knock at Miss Roger's door and in walked Big Ben along with one of his so called friends. "How can I help you?" asked Miss Rogers, surprised at seeing him, but only for a moment, for his appearance was beginning to make sense.

"I don't like to snitch on someone in my class, Miss Rogers, but for the good name of the school, I feel I have just got to," said Ben, believing her to be a rather gullible person. At this very moment the school bell rang noting the end of the lunch break. Miss Rogers now had free time and could go to the canteen for lunch, but she chose not to.

"You just go right ahead, Benjamin. I appreciate your concern for the good name of the school," said Miss Rogers, trying her best to look as serious as possible.

"Well it's like this," said Ben, doing his best to stop the grin that was beginning to spread over his face. "It's about this girl called Claire, who is in the cookery course with me. Well we both have seen her selling drugs to children just ten minutes ago in the playground and at other times too. She keeps them hidden in her school bag. Isn't that true?" he asked his friend, standing next to him.

"It certainly is true," said his lying friend, quite emphatically.

"This is very serious news indeed," cried Miss Rogers, looking quite upset. "I shall have to phone for help. A short time later one of the assistant heads arrived in the room. Miss Rogers then asked Benjamin and his friend to tell the assistant head what they had told her.

"This is a very serious matter indeed," said the assistant head, addressing Ben and his friend. "You two were quite right to report what had just happened, and I commend you for it," said the assistant head. He then sent for a guidance teacher.

When he arrived just a minute later, the assistant head explained what was going on. He told the guidance teacher to collect the young school secretary and then Claire, and bring them to the room. "This is such a serious matter, that I shall ask the deputy headteacher to join us." Ben and his friend were enjoying all this greatly, and could hardly wait to see Claire's face when she was confronted by their false allegations.

Claire was just settling into her English class when the door burst open and in came the guidance teachers. He scanned the class. "Which one of you is Claire?" he demanded to know, while completely ignoring Miss Lacey, the classroom teacher. He liked to project the attitude of being a tough guy at the expense of others.

"I am she," said Claire, and waited to find out what abuse he would fling at her.

"Collect your things, child, and put them in your school bag. The deputy head wants to see you. Make sure you leave nothing behind, for I don't think you will be returning."

"That's what you think," said Claire under her breath, and smiled.

"Get that silly grin off your face," he yelled. Claire joined him at the front of the class holding her bag. "I'll take that," he shouted at the young girl, while grabbing her bag.

He then went to leave with Claire, but found his way barred by Miss Lacey standing in front of the classroom door. "Before you leave, I just want to tell you had no business bursting into my classroom without knocking, and explaining the purpose of your visit. It is a very ill mannered and rude thing to do. Your behaviour alarmed me and also some of the children. Never behave like that again. I hope you understand, I will not put up with that sort of behaviour, no matter who it is. Do you understand?" He did not answer, but stood staring into the eyes of Miss Lacey determined to outstare the young teacher. Unfortunately for him he lost, and Miss Lacey won. She then stepped aside to let him leave along with Claire. As they were leaving Claire gazed up at Miss Lacey and smiled, who responded to Claire with a comforting smile.

The door was closed and they rejoined the young school secretary, who had been waiting for them. Claire could not help but notice he was trying his best to hide the big grin on his face, for he had heard all that had been said. "Get that smirk off your face," he snapped angrily, at the young man as they headed off to Miss Roger's room. As they made their way along the corridor, the teacher actually believed he had done a good job of enhancing his reputation of being a right tough guy, for he believed he could have easily outsmarted Miss Lacey if he had not been in such a hurry. He was soon to find out he had made a fool of himself, along with others.

CHAPTER 39
The Steadfast Miss Rogers

They soon arrived at Miss Roger's classroom and entered, while the secretary returned to work. Claire looked around the room at the collection of assembled teachers waiting to harangue her. Only Miss Rogers seemed to be on her side.

"What is this I hear of you selling drugs in the school?" the deputy headteacher asked Claire. Claire looked him up and down as if he was just some babbling idiot.

"We have proof," yelled the assistant head. "Benjamin and his friend have seen you selling them in the playground during today's lunch break. Then Big Ben and his friend repeated, with delight, their lies about Claire

"Just you go ahead child and empty your bag and pockets on to Miss Roger's desk," screamed the guidance teacher, who was not at all pleased with Claire's unruffled attitude, for he was expecting by now she would be quivering with fear and ready to burst into tears, for after all, in his twisted view, she was only a little girl. Claire did as she was told and spread the contents of her bag and pockets on the desk, including her phone. The guidance teacher raked about them, but could not find what he was looking for.

"Try in the corners of her bag," stammered Ben, not willing to believe the truth. Nothing was found by the guidance teacher, who was beginning to get upset almost as much as Ben.

"Here, let me see," cried Ben, and rushed to the bag, almost knocking the guidance teacher to the floor. He too searched the bag, but found nothing. "It's in her jacket," he screamed, while pointing a trembling finger at Claire. "I saw her take two twenty pound notes when she was selling drugs. Look for the notes. You saw her with the notes too, didn't you?" he wailed, as he looked over at his friend. His friend said nothing, for he could see the game was up.

It was now time for Miss Rogers to intervene. She sent the guidance teacher to the school office to collect the letter with the key that had been placed in the safe. When he returned with the envelope it was handed to the deputy head who then opened it to find the key. At the suggestion of Miss Rogers, he went over to her desk, opened the drawer and removed the drugs and the money. Miss Rogers then spoke. "Claire found these in her bag at the end of the cookery course lesson, and brought them to me immediately after the lunch break started. It is logged in the school office." She held them up one at a time using her tongs. Those in the room just gaped at them. "Well Benjamin, how did you manage to see Claire selling drugs in the playground just ten minutes before the end of the lunch break," asked Miss Rogers, as she looked straight at him.

"It wasn't me. I never put the drugs in that girl's bag. It was him," he cried, pointing at his so-called friend.

"Miss Rogers, could you please look at the video on my phone?" asked Claire. "It was taken during the cooking lesson, when I was at the sink." All eyes were on Miss Rogers as she viewed the video. She then handed the phone to the deputy head and the rest of them crowded around him.

CHAPTER 40

The Intrepid Miss Rogers

"This is now a police matter, Benjamin, you shall go and sit outside my office until they arrive," announced the Deputy Head. He said this just to frighten the boy, for he had no intention of involving the police, and giving the school a bad reputation. He knew that Ben would have no thought of sitting demurely alone outside his office while the police were being called. He was expecting Ben to just slip away quietly, and end up in some city on the other end of the country.

"You all can go to blazes," shrieked Big Ben. "You won't be seeing me here at this dump of a school and town ever again," he shrieked even louder, as he knocked the guidance teacher to the floor, and bulldozed aside the deputy head and the assistant head as he fled out of the room, down the corridor and out of a fire door.

They let him go, for they did not want him in their catchment area, and it suited them for they were more interested in the good name of the school than in pursuit of justice. As for Ben's lying friend, they accepted his story that he had been made to say what he said about Claire, and he was scared to disobey Ben. "You seemed to enjoy lying about Claire. Why is that?" asked Miss Rogers to Ben's friend. He just stood there looking at the floor and did not answer. The other three teachers in the room did not press him for an answer, as they wanted the whole affair to be forgotten. "You better not try that trick again boy, as long as I am in this school. Any boy who behaves like that to a young girl is such a disgusting person in my opinion. You should remember, we have you on tape. You are now dismissed." He was never again to be seen at that school. He did not flee the area for he knew the school had absolved him of lying about Claire, but at the same time he felt they would not miss him if he never returned to the school. He was spot on.

There were just two more things for them to do. They blamed Miss Rogers for not telling them straight away that she had the evidence in her drawer. They expected her to take their criticism of her without protest, but they were sadly mistaken. "I gave Benjamin and his friend enough rope to hang themselves. I completely reject your criticism of me," said a defiant Miss Rogers. That shut them up.

It was then the deputy head stepped forward and examined the two small packets of drugs. He went over to the classroom sink at the far side of the room where he carefully opened them and then with his finger he pretended to taste the contents.

He spat each time into the sink. "Just flour and bicarbonate of soda," he exclaimed. "Well I never thought that," he muttered, as he emptied the powders down the sink and washed them away. He then turned and looked at the others in the room as he shoved the empty packets into his pocket. There is now just the question of the so-called drug money. The money will go into the school funds. This has just been one big waste of time. Much ado about nothing."

"You had better go back to your class now, Claire," said Miss Rogers. You have been a very brave girl. You can sleep well tonight along with many others, for that bully will be miles away from here by tonight."

"Thank you Miss Rogers, and thank you for your kind and gentle words," said Claire, as she turned with a disapproving look upon her face and set her eyes on the other teachers in the room. Claire packed her bag and left with her head held high. The other teachers sloughed away while Miss Rogers headed for the canteen, where her meal was being kept warm in the oven.

As Claire made her way back to her class, she thanked God once again for His protection. She believed that Big Ben and his sidekick would never be seen again at the school, but she also believed that she would meet up with the pair of them again quite soon. She was soon proved to be correct.

CHAPTER 41

Back at School

Next day Big Ben and his so-called friend never turned up at school. Claire met Gwen in the playground before the school started and they had a chat. Anyone who saw Gwen chatting with Claire thought she was being rather stupid for they all knew it had been forbidden by Big Ben. A little boy, who liked Gwen very much, felt compelled to do something. "Don't you know, Gwen, that you are not allowed to talk to this girl," he said. "You better leave now just in case you get told on."

"I'm all right, Neville. "Thank you for your concern, but you don't need to worry about me."

"But…" said Neville, without managing to continue, for Claire had interrupted the small boy, who obviously had a crush on Gwen.

"He is never going to bully Gwen, or for that matter anyone else ever again at this school," said Claire. Just for only a second Claire thought she may have said too much, but she was not having Neville worry all day as to what may happen. Claire gave him a warm smile which made Neville believe what he had just heard was true. They then headed to the school entrance with Neville and Gwen feeling much happier than when they arrived.

"Is that really true just what you said that we don't need to worry about the Big Ben any more?" asked Gwen, while gazing in amazement at Claire, for she almost did believe it was true. Many in Gwen's year group had suffered for a long time from his bullying and insults that it seemed hard to believe that it had at last ended.

"Thanks to you, and the video you took of Ben going into my bag, he will probably never enter this school or any other school again. He is big enough to claim he has reached the school leaving age and get away with it. It was your video that finally scared him off. No one knows you took the video and I won't tell." Claire gave her friend a smile of assurance. Gwen now believed that it was true what Claire had told her about Ben.

It was then Claire spotted Ron and Florence also heading for the school building. Claire held back with Gwen so she could say hello to them. Claire really wanted to see if they would recognise her greeting or just ignore her altogether.

"Hello, you two, how are things going?" called out Claire, when they were just about to over take her. To her disappointment there was no reply. Claire sighed causing Gwen to look over at her and into her eyes.

"Don't give up on them, Claire," whispered Gwen, as they entered the school.

"Be assured, Gwen, I shan't," said Claire emphatically. I shall keep on praying for them," and smiled as each went their own way to their class.

At the morning interval there was still no sign of the Big Ben and again at lunch time. Gwen was pleased that she had believed what Claire had said about Big Ben was true. By the end of the week word in the school was that not only was the Big Ben missing, but so also was his dog. The most popular explanation for this was that he had gone to stay with one of his so-called uncles in some large city taking his dog along with him.

CHAPTER 42

The Maths Class

Now some time ago, on her first full day at her new school, Claire attended her Maths class. In her last school she had been moved from a mediocre class into the top class, because she had done so well in a maths inter school competition. However, the information that her new school had received about Claire was that she had come from the lower grade class, and not the top class she had been moved into. The head of maths, a Mr Leaky, assumed therefore she was what he would call, "a bit of a dummy," for he was ignorant of the fact that she was a brilliant mathematician. He had plans for Claire and knew exactly in which class to place her.

When the time came Claire went to the room marked on her time table, and presented herself to the maths' teacher, a Mr Wilson. He was not pleased at all, having a new pupil in his class. "You are expected to work hard in this class. What class were you in at your last school?"

"I was moved around," said Claire.

"It says you were in the bottom maths class"

shrieked the teacher, so that the whole class could hear. Is that correct?" He had been given the information about Claire in his pigeon hole that very morning.

"Yes, Sir," said Claire, in a firm voice, to show she was not daunted by the teacher's aggressive tone. Claire had indeed been in the bottom maths class, where she could help some others with their maths.

"You should know that this is the second top maths class in your year group, it's the B class, and I have to conclude you are only in it because the bottom class is allegedly full up. The moment I find that there is a vacancy in any lower class you will have to be moved. You better know right now that you won't be here for very long."

"I understand," said Claire, and smiled, hoping that day would arrive as soon as possible, and she would be free from this callous man.

"We are just starting a new topic, so I just hope it won't be too difficult for you. Go and sit down now," he snapped at Claire, as he had handed her a jotter and book.

"Where shall I sit, Sir?" asked Claire.

"Turn around and have a look," he growled, and dismissed her. Claire looked and found there was only one vacant seat in the whole class and that was next to a boy.

The boy smiled at Claire. "Welcome, my name's Hugh," he whispered.

"Nice to meet you, Hugh. I'm Claire," she also

whispered.

"There will be no talking in this class," scolded the teacher when he observed Claire whispering. Soon the lesson was underway and for the whole time Mr Wilson simply ignored Claire, that is until the door burst open and in walked another man.

"I have come to see how your new pupil is getting on, Mr Wilson. Where is she?"

"I am here, Sir," said Claire, as she rose to her feet.

"I never asked you child, I asked Mr Wilson. Sit down," he snarled.

"Are all the teachers in this school insensitive with no concern for the feelings of others?" Claire asked herself.

"Well, how is she doing?" Mr Wilson.

Mr Wilson turned and looked at Claire, as did Hugh sitting next to her. Hugh did not like the way that she was being treated, but was not surprised, for that was the way the Maths Department was run. In short, be as nasty as you can to the pupils and keep them in fear of the teacher.

"The girl should not be in my class, Mr Leaky. I'm surprised you placed her here. Claire took it that Mr Leaky must be the head of the maths department and she was right.

"I wanted to place her in the bottom class, Mr Wilson, or any other class, but yours was the only one with a vacancy.

"Really!" exclaimed Mr Wilson, showing he very much doubted what had just been stated.

"Yes, it really is," Mr Wilson, snarled Mr Leaky,

while grinding his teeth.

"I suppose there was no room in your class, Mr Leaky?" asked Mr Wilson, showing his contempt for what he took as a contrived situation.

Mr Leaky began to see that the situation was beginning to get out of hand, so he decided to leave."I have to return to my class now Mr Wilson, for I have another teacher looking after it. I just came to see how the new girl was doing," he said."

"As if he cared," said Claire to herself. "It is obvious they both loathe each other, they care nothing for me, and he only came into the class to rub in the fact that he was the one that was responsible for placing me with this awful teacher. No doubt they both want to get the best results in the maths exams, and do whatever they can to win. Best results means more promotions. I'm just a pawn in their ambitions."

When the lesson was over and they were leaving the classroom Hugh spoke to Claire. "I'm sorry I did not stand up and protest when the two teachers were disparaging you, Claire. I just lacked the courage."

"You have nothing to be ashamed of Hugh. In this case I believe the old saying that discretion is the better part of valour."

CHAPTER 43
The Maths Test

That was then, but now every class was meant to start and finish a topic round about the same time, and then they would all be tested on the subject. There were a bunch of tests available to use, all of the same standard of difficulty. The reason for this being that not all classes met on the same day at the same time. The teachers had to draw straws to see which test they would give.

Well the time had arrived when the test was to be given to the class that Claire was in. Now, before the test was handed to the pupils, the teacher, Mr Wilson, had an important announcement to make. "There are several vacant places waiting to be filled in the bottom class, and that is where some of you will land up if you perform badly," he said, while fixing his beady eyes on Claire for a longer time than was necessary. He then handed out the papers, and as soon as all the pupils received the test it was announced they all could begin. Claire just sat and looked at the test paper, did a little writing, folded her arms waiting for the test to finish. Hugh glanced at her from time to time and felt so sorry for her.

Two days later, the test had been marked and was now ready to be handed back to the pupils. When the class met that day Mr Wilson could hardly wait to return the test papers to the children to go over it. "As is the custom I shall begin with the pupil with the top mark and work my way down to the bottom mark," as he looked at Claire with a nice big grin on his face. The top mark turned out to be ninety six percent by a girl, and that girl was not Claire. Mr Wilson kept returning the papers and calling out the marks until he came to a boy who had scored seventy five percent. "I had expected a better mark from you," he told the boy. "Next time we have a test I want to see some improvement."

He now had just two more papers to hand back. He went up to Hugh and slammed down his paper on the desk. "Thirty one percent! Disgraceful," he shouted, "but not nearly as bad as this girl sitting next to you." He went up to Claire's desk and towering over her he waved her paper in the air. "Five percent," was all he said, as he dropped the paper on her desk, and walked back to the teacher's desk with such disdain, that would make most believe he had been sucking an extremely sour lemon.

When the bell rang and they left the classroom Hugh approached Claire. "I thought you would do better than that, Claire," hoping that Claire had some explanation for her dismal mark,

"And I thought the same about you too, Hugh. Is

it for the same reason I had to get out of that class, and away from that repulsive Mr Wilson?" asked Claire. "Like me, did you not try to pass the test, because you wanted out of that awful class?"

"Yes it was," admitted Hugh, surprised Claire had found him out. However, Hugh had a much better reason for flunking the test, it was simply that he wanted to be with Claire.

Next time the maths class met Claire and Hugh were sent off to Miss Ashton's class which was the bottom maths class, and did not follow the same curriculum as the other classes. Claire knocked at the door of the classroom, where they were welcomed in by the teacher, who was expecting them. "Just sit over there," said Miss Ashton, pointing out two empty places next to each other, with a motion of her hand. "The two boys that sat there won't be returning," said Miss Ashton, looking straight at Claire. "I want you both to feel at home here and work hard." When Claire was seated she looked up at Miss Ashton with her eyes wide open, wondering just how much she knew about the incident with Big Ben, for she had often seen Miss Rogers and Miss Ashton sitting together in the canteen. "I can assure you Claire, that this is where you will be sitting as long as you are in my class," said Miss Ashton, looking straight at Claire.

CHAPTER 44
The Young Mathematician

Miss Ashton then addressed the whole class and the lesson started. Claire really enjoyed the lesson and even answered some of the questions that had been asked. It was certainly a relief not having to face the obnoxious Mr Wilson.

As they were leaving the classroom and about to head off to the canteen, Miss Ashton asked Claire to just wait a moment at the door. When they were alone she spoke to Claire. "I just wanted to tell you Claire not to worry, for that Ben, oops, that boy and his friend will never be returning to this school." Miss Ashton had been shocked when she first saw Claire enter her room. She could hardly believe that this little girl was the one Miss Rogers had told her about, the one that had stood up to Ben and his friend. She wanted to assure Claire that she was now quite safe. "If you have any problems Claire, just see me or my colleague, Miss Rogers. Claire thanked her for her concern about her safety.

Miss Aston had been honest with her, but Claire now felt that she had not been a hundred percent honest with Miss Ashton. Could you please give me just five minutes of your time, Miss?" asked Claire.

"How can I help you, Claire?" asked Miss Ashton, wondering what revelation Claire was about to unveil.

"Could you please show me a maths book with some really hard questions to solve. The more difficult the better?" asked Claire.

"Certainly," said Miss Ashton. She went to her desk and produced a book of maths problems for A| grade students.

"Could you please now pick a problem for me to solve." Miss Ashton opened the book and selected the most difficult one she could find, for she was getting slightly annoyed at Claire, thinking she was playing some silly joke on her.

Claire took her jotter out of her bag, picked up the book and sat down at one of the desks in the class. Miss Ashton watched Claire scribbling away and was not amused. She began to think she had been mistaken in her assessment of this girl's character, and was just about to tell Claire she had put up with her silly behaviour long enough, when all of a sudden Claire jumped up from her seat announcing she had finished, and had solved the problem. Claire then handed Miss Ashton her book back and showed her working in the jotter. Miss Ashton sat down and studied Claire's workings. She just could not believe what had happened, for all that Claire had written down was correct. "Would you like me to solve another problem, Miss?" asked Claire.

"Yes," said Miss Ashton, almost lost in a daze as she selected another problem to solve. She handed Claire a piece of foolscap from her drawer and Claire went to work again solving it, but with Miss Ashton standing over her watching her work. It was only when Miss Ashton had seen Claire at work, that she believed it was not some kind of joke.

"Please don't tell anyone. It was just to get away from Mr Wilson that I had to deceive you. Please forgive me. I thought I could help others in this class."

"There is nothing to forgive, Claire," said Miss Ashton.

"I'm worried about Hugh," Miss Ashton. "I never knew Hugh was of the same mind. He must have seen me looking lost in the test, and decided he also was going to fail." Claire paused and looked into the kind face of Miss Ashton. "Please don't send us back to Mr Wilson's class, please Miss Ashton," pleaded Claire, with her words and her eyes.

"Of course I shan't," replied Miss Ashton, with firm resolve. She knew of Mr Wilson's reputation of being a rather nasty person, but what she had now learned about Claire and Hugh deliberately failing a test just to get away from him, really shocked her. She wondered how many other children had done the same thing.

"What would you like me to do, Claire?" asked Miss Ashton.

"If it's possible could you please arrange for Hugh to be placed in a class that follows the curriculum when a vacancy occurs, and as for me could I please stay in your class, so I could perhaps be of some help to others when we work in groups?"

"Now that is a good idea," said Miss Wilson, "I can get that done." She then paused and looked very thoughtful. "The only flaw I see in your solution is that Hugh may want to stay sitting side by side with you in my class," said Miss Ashton, with a mischievous smile on her lips.

"Why *really*, Miss Ashton!" cried Claire, with a hint of scolding in her voice. They both laughed. It was now time to leave so Claire headed for the canteen leaving Miss Ashton to lock up. She did so, but not before placing the foolscap paper with Claire's workings safely in her desk drawer.

CHAPTER 45
They Ought to have Known Better

A strange thing happened to Claire one day in the gym dressing room. Now before entering the gym hall, Claire would hang her school clothes up on her peg, and then put on her gym kit. Well as usual after the lesson the class would go back into the changing room and get back into their school things. However, that day it so happened Claire noticed that the white school shirt that hung on her peg was not the one she had hung there at the start of the lesson. It was the same size as hers, and it looked the same, but Claire definitely knew it was not hers. Anyway she did put it on as if it was indeed her shirt, but at the same time she surveyed the expression on the other girls' faces. There was one that had a smirk of complete contentment on her little innocent looking face, and on seeing it Claire had just to smile, for Claire had often seen that very girl chatting to Big Ben in the playground. "The pieces of the jigsaw are beginning to fit together," said Claire to herself.

This reminded Claire of an old Sherlock Holmes' story. It told of a young man in a hotel, who one evening, left a pair of boots outside his door to be cleaned, to find in the morning just one boot instead of two. Claire concluded that someone was planning to kill her, and she now knew how it was going to be carried out. It would not be an attempt to be run down by a car, or to be met by a gang of thugs, or someone with a knife on her way home. "No, I shall be attacked by a dog, and that dog will have my sent," said Claire to herself. "Wouldn't it be a coincidence if it indeed turned out to be a hound as in the story." Claire there and then thanked God for warning her of the approaching danger.

Just a few days after that on her way home from school, Claire had reached the part of her homeward journey where she could either take the hill road leading to home, or take the dirt path to the field that used to lead to the now missing bridge. There was now no choice, but to use the hill road, or so Claire thought before things started to evolve.

Just a short distance from the hill road there was a car parked at the side of the street where there had never been a parked car before. Claire noted that fact and ventured cautiously on her way. As she was about to pass by the car, the driver's window rolled down and a familiar head stuck out. "Hey, I bet you never expected to see us ever again." It was Big Ben along with his so-called friend which was no surprise to Claire, for she certainly was expecting to meet the pair of them again.

They were laughing and sneering at the young girl thinking just how clever they were to have found her. Claire looked into the car, and there in the backseat was his sidekick, who in one hand was holding Claire's lost school shirt, while in the other hand a dog leash attached to what to Claire looked like an attack dog.

Claire just fled from them as fast as she could, for she knew that they had come to kill her. If they had just kept quiet they would have had a much better chance in killing her, but that they just could not do. Every day since that day they left the school their hatred for Claire had just grown more and more, until they just had to act. The hour of revenge was at hand. They were indeed there to kill her, but they so much wanted Claire to know before she died, that they were the ones who would bring her young life to an end. The pair of them had, what only could be described as, Claire derangement syndrome.

CHAPTER 46
Yet Another Tragedy

They had done their homework on Claire, for they had asked their friends at school to find out about the route Claire took on her journey home each day from school and what was the quietest part of the journey. They expected Claire now to take the street to the hill road and there the attack dog would do what it had been trained to do, and they would be there with their phones to record it. They had hired the dog for the day and had paid a lot of money for the privilege of doing so. Unfortunately for them their expectation was wrong, for Claire had made off down the path to the field and not the street to the hill road.

When Claire reached the field she had already gained quite a distance between herself and those in the car. Big Ben had driven as fast as he could along the dirt road, but he could have gone far quicker on a proper tarmac road. He was quite surprised when he came to the grass field, for he never knew this field existed or that there was a river running through it. To him that would be the countryside and he wanted nothing to do with it.

It was then the back door of the car was opened, and the thug holding the dog did his best to get out of the vehicle along with the dog. It was one thing the thug had not rehearsed and he made a mess of it, giving Claire an even bigger lead. When he was eventually ready to release the dog, he gave it one more sniff at the shirt and let it off the leash, as he pointed to Claire while giving it the command to kill. Off it went like a rocket, as the thug got back into the car. Then off went the car with Ben driving, and the other thug in the back seat, with his head and arm leaning out the rear window, still holding Claire's shirt in his hand while waving it in the air like some battle flag.

The attack dog had already made up a lot of ground on Claire, and now the two thugs were convinced that if the dog did not kill her in the field, it would surely catch up on Claire if she decided to flee up the hill which she seemed to be heading for. They grinned from ear to ear as they imagined capturing every moment of her death on their phones.

There was now Claire running to get to the river crossing, the dog running behind her with the thugs in the car following on going faster and faster. The thug in the back of the car kept shouting obscenities at Claire and encouraging the dog to kill. It was a flat field, so Big Ben felt emboldened to increase his speed in order to get closer and closer to the action. Now when Claire arrived at the narrowest part of the river she kept on running if there was no river there at all. She easily leapt across the river with the dog following on. The dog had no clue what was happening and landed in the river and was swept away.

Big Ben, while still thinking of the agony that Claire would be soon going through, never heard the roar of the river above the revving up of the car engine as he put his foot down hard on the accelerator. He had forgotten all about the dog, for his eyes were firmly fixed on Claire as she was now making her way up the grassy hill. There was no escape for her now. "Gotcha," he shouted in glee as the car crashed into the river and disappeared from view.

Claire ran and looked over the bank and down into the water. There was nothing to see, except a maple leaf being swept along on the river, and there on the edge of the river at the foot of the steep bank, caught in a tangled web of vegetation, Claire noticed a white cotton piece of cloth with a collar attached. It was doing its best to be set free to be allowed to drift down the river to the ocean, just like that maple leaf. Claire bowed her head and thanked God once again for her deliverance. She then plodded home up the hill with many a sigh as she thought over the waste of another two lives.

That night in her prayers Claire also remembered the dog and how it had been abused by wicked people who had turned it into an attack dog, and she asked The Lord to help those who were trying to end this evil trade. The strange thing was that when she had crossed the river and turned and looked at the dog, she found that it was indeed a hound. "How strange is that?" she said in wonder.

CHAPTER 47
The Rehearsal

One day after school, when Claire was chatting with Mrs Fisher, she asked Claire if she could find out if Emily could come to a rehearsal of the quartet on Saturday afternoon at three. "May I come to the rehearsal also?" asked Claire. "I could also be a stand in if someone is absent on the day."

"Of course you may, Claire," said Mrs Fisher, with some sympathy for Claire, who she believed was hardly proficient in playing the piano or singing. It was an unjustified notion that had somehow entered her mind for some reason or other. "I think you will learn a lot and will enjoy the experience," she told Claire, to comfort the young girl.

When Claire met Emily the next day, Emily accepted the invitation. "The only thing I am worried about on the day of the show," said Emily, "is that a group of troublemakers, and a certain bully may find out about my part in the show, and come and cause trouble. I shan't let that stop me though."

"Good for you, Emily," said Claire.

By three o'clock on Saturday they all were

gathered together in Mrs Fisher's house in the music room. Claire had been the last to arrive and when she walked into the room she was greeted by a surprised cries of delight by Mrs Hay the violinist and Miss Willow, the cellist. "We both are delighted to see you once again, Claire. We never knew you were acquainted with Mrs Fisher. We so much enjoyed listening to you that day."

"How is your dog doing after that dreadful incident, Miss Willow?" Now Miss Willow could talk all day about her dog, and Claire knew it. Claire just asked to divert her talking about playing and singing just in case they might compare Claire with Emily. She told Claire it was doing fine. "You may be wondering why I am here, well I have come to learn about playing the piano and singing in public halls and care homes. I'm sure I shall learn a lot and perhaps one day I can do the same. Claire lowered her head a little to one side and studied the faces of both ladies to see if they got the message. They got it, and there was no more talk about Claire the pianist and singer.

Claire was then introduced to the other violinist, Mr Beatty, by Mrs Fisher.

"It's nice to meet you, Mr Beatty," said Claire.

"And you too," said Mr Beatty, as they shook hands. "If you like you may call me Mr Bee, Claire. It's spelt bee."

"Are you a beekeeper then?" asked Claire.

"Yes, I am, Claire," he answered, impressed that she had worked out the riddle at the first attempt.

"When I retired I took up beekeeping and have several hives throughout my garden."

"I think I pass your house when going to and returning from school, for I have noticed one large house with several bee hives in the front garden," said Claire." Claire turned out to be correct.

"He produces excellent honey, apart from being an accomplished violinist," said Mrs Fisher. "Not only that, he is the President of our local Wild Birds Preservation Society, and has many bird feeders, bird tables and baths in his garden.

The rehearsal went well. Emily sang beautifully and the instrumentalist performed splendidly. The show would take place next Saturday in the local church hall.

"How do you think we should end the show," asked Miss Willow.

"Since we are in a church I think we should end with singing a hymn," suggested Mrs Hay. "Mrs Fisher could play the piano and I have already heard Claire sing one of my favourite hymns. Would you sing it for us Claire, at the close of the concert?" Claire was quite surprised at the request and of course accepted the invitation to sing. The meeting then ended and all those present were given tickets to sell for the concert in the church hall. Claire was glad she had attended the rehearsal, for she felt she had learned a lot about small local concerts.

CHAPTER 48
Claire Sells a Ticket

Now on her way home on Tuesday from school Claire had to pass by Mr Beatty's house. He was working at his beehives and when he saw Claire he left them and came to speak to Claire, to find out how the tickets were selling. "I haven't managed to sell a single ticket," Claire told him. "Have you sold any Mr Beatty?" It turned out he had sold quite a lot to his group of friends, the news of which cheered up Claire.

Finally that day Claire thought she might be able to sell a ticket to Miss Sipps. She soon got the opportunity. While her mother was washing dishes in the scullery the servants' bell rang. When Claire turned up to answer the call she got a dirty look from Mrs Sipps when she knocked and entered the sitting room. She told Claire to draw the curtains which she did, but as usual she was not quite satisfied with the result and got Claire to fiddle about with them just to try and annoy the young girl.

It was then Claire made her big mistake, which later turned out to be for the good, by asking

Mrs Sipps if she would like to buy a ticket to the Concert in the Church hall in which Claire would sing. Claire was trying to be nice to Mrs Sipps in the hope that she would perhaps change her ways. To Claire's surprise she bought a ticket and dismissed Claire. Claire's heart sank as she walked slowly back to the kitchen, as the truth dawned on her. "She has bought the ticket so that when my mum asks for time off to go to the concert she will refuse, because the house would be left empty which Mrs Sipps would not allow," said Claire to herself. "In her mind she will now think she has a just cause to stop my mother attending. When she got back to the scullery Claire told her mother what had happened.

"Don't worry Claire," she said in a gentle voice. "Just remember, *we know that all things work together for good to them that love God.*" Claire's mum actually did ask Mrs Sipps for time off to see her daughter in the concert, and as expected was refused.

CHAPTER 49
The Church Hall Show

They came together again next Saturday in a local church hall. Mrs Hay had invited Abigail and Ruth to attend, and she asked Claire to go with them. Claire was not too happy about Ruth attending for she felt there was going to be trouble at the show, and both Abigail and Ruth had had their fair share of trouble recently. On the other hand she knew Abigail, like Emily, was not going to let the bullies ruin their lives. It was only for a fleeting second that the thought that perhaps they should not attend, had entered Claire's mind, so she dismissed it right away.

When they were ready to start an audience of about seventy had assembled. They were of all ages, but they had one thing in common, they were all in some way linked to the members of the quartet. Emily had actually persuaded some of her friends to attend, but unfortunately, some others who were anything but her friends had gotten wind of what was happening, and were now in the audience. Just before the show began Emily looked through the curtains at the side of the stage to view the audience. "All my friends are there. I'm so glad they all have turned up to support me," said Emily to Claire, who was at her side. When she had closed the gap in the curtain she gave out a muffled cry and opened the gap once more. "Oh no, he's there," she told Claire, with the sound of her voice showing some distress.

Claire looked through the curtain. "Back row, four from the left flanked by a couple of his pals?" asked Claire. Emily nodded. Claire had seen him at school, and had learned he was the senior bully of the school now that Big Ben had gone.

"They call him Slippery Sam. He doesn't like me," said Emily. "I have reported him, but nothing has been done about it. His father is a big shot, owning several large stores, and smaller convenient stores in the town. The school is frightened to confront him. I think his family approve of his bullying, believing it builds up his character, and makes him ready for the world of business. What other explanation can there be?"

"I shall keep an eye on him, Emily. Dismiss him from your mind and forget he's there."

"But will he forget that I am there," asked Emily.

"Let's see if he does," said Claire, and smiled. Emily sighed, for in her heart she believed that in no way could a little girl like Claire could help. She felt the inevitable would happen, namely Slippery Sam would ruin her performance. They parted. Claire went to join the audience while Emily went backstage to wait.

The show started with a senior mixed choir singing some old songs. Next the quartet appeared and played some favourite melodies. All the time Claire was at the back of the hall keeping an eye on the three bullies. Claire could see that they were becoming restless having to listen to music having no continuous beat. "If only there was the sound of a dripping tap right now, to go along with the music, I suppose they would be quite happy. The beat must be like a drug to them," said Claire to herself.

Then it was time for the choir to perform again. It had become all too much for one of the bullies, for the chief Sam left his seat and started to walk to and fro at the back of the hall, leaving his sidekicks squirming in their seats. Claire, who had made sure she was not seen by hiding in the shadows, had changed her appearance using disguises from her backpack.

Claire noticed that when Sam vacated his seat he had lifted a plastic bag from the floor and left it on his seat. "Probably to make sure he does not step on it when he returns," reasoned Claire to herself. "I bet it's full of a selection of rotten eggs, tomatoes and fruit, ready to be thrown when Emily appears on stage. Most likely than not, the other two have similar bags, filled with the same rotting stuff from one of his father's stores."

CHAPTER 50

Claire takes Action

The time for Emily to sing had now arrived, so Sam returned to his seat. Emily walked onto the stage along with the quartet, and they took up their positions with Emily right in the middle at the front of the stage, as close to the audience as possible. "That is just the kind of a target a bully loves," thought Claire, who was now positioned behind the three of them.

As Emily started to sing the bullies were ready to get up from their seats, but suddenly they had their chairs pulled away from under them. They went crashing to the floor. They lay there just for a few seconds wondering what on earth had happened, before struggling to their feet still gripping their bags. It was when they got to their feet, they heard a laugh and saw a little girl pointing and laughing at them. "What have you got in your bags?" she asked them."

"You're just about to find out," screamed Sam, as he dipped into his bag and brought out an egg ready to throw at her. The other two were doing the same, the only difference was that one had a tomato and the other a rotten apple. They were so full of hate for the girl they did not realise that the whole audience had turned round and were looking at them. The first to throw was the chief Sam, but he completely missed. The stage performance ended. The audience gave out a cry of horror as they saw the egg on its way to the little girl followed by a sigh of relief as it missed her, and crashed against the wall. The other two bullies saw this as a chance to show their leader what they could do, and be heroes, but they missed too. The three of them kept on trying to hit Claire until it entered their thick heads that it was just not going to happen.

Casting away his bag the leader made a rush at Claire, again followed by his two obsequious helpers. They were never going to catch Claire, but it would take several minutes for that to sink into their stupid heads. Meanwhile, the lights had been switched on with the audience now watching what was going on. Some were standing and cheering while others were sitting and clapping, all doing their best to support the girl. At last the three gave up the chase and for the first time realised that they were being watched.

Mr Beatty, who had been standing on the stage watching what had been going on, decided to give them a piece of his mind. "You three thugs, just get out of here immediately," he roared. "You're a disgrace, attacking a little girl. Now just leave."

"Steady on Grandpa," said Slippery Sam looking

straight at Mr Beatty. "The girl is a troublemaker, about to disrupt your show. We came in here to stop her. She had brought stuff to throw at the stage. At least we stopped her."

"No one believes a single word of that. The three of you came here to disrupt the show, and the girl prevented you," said Mr Beatty, in a strong authoritative voice. "Just go."

"Why don't you shut up and buzz off you old fool," snarled the bully, with a smirk on his face, thinking he was making a fool out of Mr Beatty. Claire could not but notice the use of the word buzz,

which suggested to her that Sam knew Mr Beatty kept bees.

Slippery Sam looked around the hall expecting to see the audience giggling and smiling, but that they were certainly not doing that. He was digging a hole for himself that he was not going to get out of. He realised it was time to go. "Let's get out of here," he called out to his two companions. "These folk are just a bunch of losers." He swaggered to the door followed by his two goons, and they left not bothering to close the door behind them. The audience watched them leave and then turned round to see what was happening on the stage, and found Mr Beatty still standing alone at the front of the stage where he received their spontaneous cheer.

CHAPTER 51
The Show Goes on

Meanwhile, the little girl had slipped along the side of the hall unseen and through a small door and into a passage that had steps up to the stage. The cheering had now stopped, and now she heard a lady address the audience and recognised the voice of Mrs Fisher. Claire removed her wig and a couple of garments and returned to being Claire, the only difference being she was now carrying her back pack. She retraced her steps, rejoined Abigail and Ruth and listened to Mrs Fisher who had persuaded everyone in the hall to agree to carry on the show and forget about what had just happened. Meanwhile, Mr Beatty had left the stage, closed the door of the hall and had retrieved the three bags of rot that the thugs had brought with them.

When Mrs Fisher had finished talking Mr Beatty held up the three bags. "We all know who brought in the bags and why they did it," said Mr Beatty, to a cheer from all. He looked around to the audience to find the girl, but was disappointed to find she had left. "The girl has left," he told the audience.

"I reckon she must be rather modest, but whoever she was we thank her." Another cheer rang out. "The show must go on," he said, and that is exactly what happened, and who was the star of the show, well that turned out to be none other than Emily. Claire had asked Emily to take her place in singing the closing hymn, just in case anyone in the audience spotted some resemblance between herself and the heroic girl.

It was just after four o'clock when they all had left the hall and Mr Beatty locked it up. The quartet plus Emily drove off in Mr Beatty's car with Miss Willow's cello safely in the boot. Claire said goodbye to them for she had decided to accompany Abigail and Ruth back to their home and off they went. Mrs Hay watched them leave.

Now Ruth would sometimes run ahead of them and then stand and wait for them to catch. On one such occasion, Abigail asked Claire the big question that was on her mind. She stopped walking which caused Claire also to stop. "Claire," said Abigail, looking Claire straight in the eye, "was that you, the girl that these thugs were attacking?"

Claire said not a word, so they walked on together, as Claire thought of how best to answer her friend. Then Claire spoke. "I think it's better if you don't know who it was. If anyone thinks you may know the answer, you can say you don't know who it was without wondering if you should lie or not. Abigail, I do think it's best you don't know."

"You are right, Claire. On Monday at school, when

these three toughs are bound to see me, then they will surely be questioning me. It's best, as you say, that I don't know. I should never have asked."

"Don't worry, I would have probably asked too," said Claire.

Now to get Abigail safely home they had to pass Miss Willow's house where Miss Willow and the rest of the quartet , along with Emily were now having afternoon tea. Miss Willow was looking out of the sitting room window when she spotted Claire, Abigail and Ruth, and went out and invited them to join them for afternoon tea, an invitation that they accepted gladly. Before the three girls started eating Mr Beatty rose to his feet, just ahead of Claire who had the same desire, and thanked God for their deliverance from the thugs and for the safety of the young heroine. He then thanked God once again for the food that lay before them. As he sat down he glanced at Claire wondering just who this girl really was.

CHAPTER 52

Gang Revenge

Now Claire believed that sooner or later Slippery Sam and his lackeys would try to inflict revenge on Mr Beatty. She believed they knew he was a beekeeper, and that he probably had beehives in his garden. "What could be an easier revenge for them than to topple over his hives," said Claire to herself. "I don't think that they will be seeking revenge today, for they probably have had enough excitement for one day" thought Claire. Tomorrow is Sunday and Sam will probably be looking forward to the family lunch of roast beef. No, I think it will be after school on Monday, when the three of them are gathered together again that they will seek retribution for their humiliation at the hands of Mr Beatty."

On Monday after school, Claire set off to Mr Beatty's mansion and hid among the bushes on the waste land on the other side of the street to Mr Beatty's house. She knew she would probably encounter some bees, so she put on her homemade bee protection outfit which she removed from her backpack. She did not have to wait very long to find out that her prediction had been correct. There they were, the three bullies, Slippery Sam and his two faithful followers, swaggering along the road as if the street belonged to them. There was no traffic to be seen as it was a cul-de-sac with a small footpath at the other end. Mr Beatty's house was a large detached house as were all the other houses in the street. It was right at the end of the street, with a sizable front garden, in a quiet area well away from its neighbour. The three bullies looked entirely out of place when they arrived at Mr Beatty's garden gate. As the gate was wide open, and there was no car in the driveway, the three delinquents concluded, in this case correctly, that there was no one at home.

They scanned the garden with their eyes until Sam pointed out a beehive, at the far side of the garden well away from the road and the driveway. The three of them ran across the front lawn and up to the beehive. One of them must have drawn the short straw, for he had been given the task of recording the vandalism on Slippery Sam's phone. Sam with his helper removed the bricks from off the flat top of the hive, lifted the hive up as high as they could and then let go of the hive with a push so it smashed against the ground. The thug recording the video then got them to pose among the smashed-up hive then took a quick selfie of himself with the other two standing next to the destruction they had just caused. He then gave the phone back to Sam.

With mission accomplished the three errant school boys, for that's what they were, stood and looked around the garden for another beehive to smash up. All three of them had a big smirk on their face thinking, no doubt, that they had done something most noble. They had no inkling of what was about to happen to them. Meanwhile, Claire from her hiding place had also recorded what had just happened on her phone, and kept on videoing for she knew the revenge of the bees was about to take place.

The three silly vandals then began to leave, but before they had taken a step they suddenly seemed to be surrounded by bees. They had been so consumed with vanity that they had failed to notice the bees emerging from the smashed up hive.

CHAPTER 53
The Bees' Revenge

They were now encircled with bees, and the sound of their buzzing was beginning to really scare them. They started to run and swipe at the bees which did not help, for it only made the bees more and more aggressive. Now that they were getting stung they began to panic. When Sam got stung, unfortunately for him, he dropped his phone and kept running towards the gate without stopping to pick it up, probably not even knowing he had dropped it. When they reached the gate they ran to the end of the street, then along the footpath into a field which led them to another street.

Meanwhile, Claire, now with her safety outfit on, left her hiding place, crossed the road to the gate, and raced across the lawn to where the bees were, found the phone and returned to her hiding place. As she waited to see what would happen next, she copied Sam's video onto her own phone.

When the three thugs stopped running they decided that the only sensible thing was to go back to their homes, and treat their bee stings. Just as they were about to set off Sam, who was the last to handle the phone, suddenly began to tremble. "I have dropped the phone," he shrieked. "I've dropped it." This was devastating news to the other two who stopped and stared incredulously at Sam. For a moment they just stood there speechless, then they began to scream, swear and insult him. It was the beginning of the end of the gang of three.

What had just happened had scared them more than the bees, for they knew what was on the phone could incriminate them all, so they just had to go back and find it. They searched and searched, and rang Sam's phone, but of course could not find it. They began blaming each other and the whole thing nearly broke into a fist fight, and was only prevented by the return of Mr Beatty in his car. The three of them took flight, each heading for their own home.

When Mr Beatty got out of his car he was horrified at what he found. As he stared at the smashed up hive he heard the voice of a girl behind him. "Excuse me Mr Beatty, it is I, Claire." He looked at the young girl in astonishment, as Claire explained her presence. She gave him the dropped phone and offered to help tidy up. He thanked Claire, but explained how dangerous it could be and told Claire he would be very careful. Claire then went on her way home, having received from him the promise that he would keep her name out of the whole affair.

That very evening Mr Beatty drove to the home of

Samuel and asked to speak to Sam's father. He was shown by the maid into the study, where sat the father behind an oak desk. Mr Beatty showed the father the incriminating video, and demanded he pay for the damage done to the hives. "I'm so sorry this happened to you," said the father, "and I'll make sure my son behaves himself from now on. He then took out a bundle of cash from a drawer in his desk, and laid it on top of the desk. "I think, Mr Bee, there is enough money there to buy your silence and fix your hives. I don't want to see my son with a criminal record, so I shall do my best to keep him on the right path."

The father then got out of his seat, picked up the bundle of notes and walked over to Mr Beatty," and so said went to hand Mr Bee the bundle. Now if you just give me Sam's phone we shall all be happy. Mr Bee handed him the phone believing he was sincere. He was anything but honest, for he withdrew his outstretched hand with the bundle of notes and took a few steps back. "Now get out of here you silly old man, and never try to blackmail ever again. Get out and go back to your bees."

"I have just been made to look like a fool," said Mr Beatty to himself, and turned and left.

As he walked down the corridor to the front door, the boy's father went to the study door to watch him leave. "You can see yourself out, you old codger and remember to close the door," shouted the father with a loud voice full of hate. "Buzz off back home," he added in a cruel voice, followed by a nasty sounding laugh, thinking he had just said something smart.

Next day Mr Beatty phoned the police and reported the crime. They never turned up to see the smashed up beehive, but gave him a crime number, and told him just to claim it on his insurance. Unfortunately he was not insured for such a situation.

CHAPTER 54
Indisputable Evidence

A few days later, Claire on her way home from school, went to have a look at Mr Beatty's front garden to find out if the hives had been replaced. She found Mr Beatty in his front garden attending to the new hive. When he saw Claire he went to the garden gate, where they had a most interesting chat. He told Claire all about his meeting with the bully's father and how he had been accused of black mailing him. "I was lucky enough to have left that house without being assaulted, Claire," explained Mr Beatty. "They really are a dangerous bunch of crooks, for now he has the audacity of sending me a letter saying if I persist in such unfounded allegations he will sue me."

"That is just awful!" exclaimed Claire. "Now you mention it, I have often seen photos of him advertising something or other, when I go into his shops, and now I must admit he does look like a gangster. Don't do anything just now, Mr Beatty, for I shall watch what his son gets up to in school tomorrow," said Claire, and left before Mr Beatty could object.

Next day Claire managed to waylay Sam in the playground as he was making his way to the canteen. He had no idea who this little girl was who wanted a word and told her to get lost. "You may want to know I have a video of you and your two friends smashing up a beehive. Would you like to see it?" He stopped in his tracts, turned round, and walked up slowly towards Claire. "Let's go to a quiet part of the playground," suggested Claire and off she went. He followed.

"Show me this so-called video, you have," demanded Slippery Sam, when they arrived. Claire held up her phone and when he got close enough to see told him to stop. He laughed at her request, but surprisingly for him he stopped. Claire started to run the video and the thug just stood and looked on. He actually began to shake somewhat when he saw it was genuine, and even more so when he realised he could easily be identified in it. He just had to act, he would not be stopped as he sprang at Claire hoping to grab hold of her phone. With her free hand she got hold of his outstretched hand at the wrist, spun him around a hundred and eighty degrees on his feet, then let go of him. He went tripping on his way for a few metres until his balance gave way and he fell to the ground. "Just tell your father about this video, then say if both of you cause any more trouble for Mr Bee the video will go to the police," said Claire, as he struggled to his feet.

He did not go to the canteen or attend school

that afternoon, but visited the school's nurse telling her he was not feeling well. He actually did not look well after his humiliation, so he was given leave to go home. When the school broke up Claire noticed a sinister man walking slowly past the school gates dressed in a long coat, scarf, a trilby hat and dark glasses. It seemed now that Claire was not the only one into changing their appearance, for Claire recognised him as none other than Slippery Sam. "The silly boy should have changed his shoes," whispered Claire to herself. When Claire had said goodbye to her friends she headed home followed by Sam. Having gathered all the information he needed about the route Claire was taking, he stopped tailing her and went his own way. He had stopped following Claire at the foot of the hill that led to her home which turned out to be a big mistake.

He had done a clumsy job of tracking Claire, for Claire knew she was being followed from the beginning outside the school until he stopped on the road at the foot of the hill. He had returned home thinking he had done a good job. "Something is going to happen on the road up the hill tomorrow, either on my way to school or on my way home," said Claire, to a squirrel hurrying across the road from the trees on one side of the road to those on the other. Tomorrow Claire will be proved to be right.

CHAPTER 55
Tragedy on the Hill

When Claire left the house the next day she was on full alert and had prayed that very morning for God's help to keep her safe. In her hand she held a small mirror that would help her see what was happening behind her back. When she had left the driveway of the house, and entered the road she noticed a red car parked on the side of the hill at the very top of the hill. She now knew that she would soon be attacked. She could see the car was empty, but she now suspected that whoever owned the car was hiding in the bushes next to it, just waiting for her appearance.

As she walked down the road she glanced now and again into her little mirror, and spotted two people emerge from the bushes and jump into the car. She did not know that in their hurry, caused by their hatred of Claire, they had forgotten to put on their seat belts. They started the engine and off they went down the hill on their fatal journey. Claire, of course with her remarkable hearing, heard the engine start, followed by the revving up of the engine. She walked on looking in the mirror, and just at the right moment turned to see the red car hurtling towards her picking up speed as it went. She could now look through the windscreen to find out who was in the car, and what she saw almost shocked her in losing concentration, for in the car was Sam with his father at the wheel. Just at the right moment she dived to the right, into the wood. The driver who had his eyes fixed on the little girl, automatically followed her movements as his foot pressed further down on the accelerator. Unfortunately for him and his passenger the car went crashing into a tall pine tree scattering a horde of crows that had been perching on its branches. Petrol was flowing from the car so Claire left the scene of carnage as fast as she could. Suddenly there was one loud explosion causing glass and metal to fly everywhere. Claire dived for cover and then when she deemed it to be safe, ran as fast as she could down the hill and then into the path that led to the cul-de-sac where Mr Beatty stayed. In the distance she could hear the sound of several sirens, gradually getting louder and louder.

The sound of the explosion brought people out of their houses and into their gardens trying to find out what was happening. Now Mr Beatty was one of those people and when he saw Claire making her usual morning journey to school, went down to the garden gate to see her. He waved over to Claire so she came over to see him. "Do you know what the explosion was all about?" he asked Claire.

"A car went off the road and crashed into a tree. Don't tell anyone until it is made official, that a father and son were in the car. I can tell you this for sure Mr Beatty, you don't have to be worried any longer about being sued or having your beehives trashed. I take no delight in telling you that." Mr Beatty seemed to be struck dumb by what he had just learned. Claire went on her way and Mr Beatty went back indoors.

It was not until the next morning on the news that the two bodies in the car had been identified and made public. "So Claire was right!" exclaimed Mr Beatty, when he heard the news that morning about a tragic accident that had killed a father and son. He turned off his radio and sat down at the kitchen table to think. After about ten minutes of contemplation, he suddenly jumped to his feet and cried out loud. "They were trying to murder her. They were trying to murder that little girl with a hit and run accident when she was on her way down the hill to school. Thank you God that they failed." Trembling, he sat back down and thanked God once more for keeping her safe. "How they must have hated Claire," he said, when he at last left the kitchen. As the day wore on he realised that Claire had put herself in the path of danger because of him.

On her way home from school that day, when Claire was about to pass by Mr Beatty's house, she found him waiting for her at the garden gate. He had something to tell Claire and by the look on his face it must have been something serious.

"Claire," he said, looking her straight in the eye, "any time you or your mother need help contact me, and I shall see what I can do. There is a servants' bungalow at the back of my house that is unoccupied. Remember that and tell your mum." He then gave Claire his phone number, which Claire right there entered into her phone, then thanked Mr Beatty. That was all that needed to be said and done, so Claire went on her way. That evening Mr Beatty received a text on his phone which read as follows. "My mum also thanks you. Best wishes, Claire."

CHAPTER 56
The Local Bird Count

Four times every year on Saturdays, the local Bird Society would hold a bird count. It was very popular among the members for it brought a lot of them together for the day. One day they would count garden birds then a week later woodland birds. Of course, the weather on the count days had to be the same as it was on the last count three months ago. Mrs Fisher invited Claire and Abigail, who were members of the society, to a sleepover on the day of the evening count. After obtaining permission from their family they accepted.

The garden bird count went well and next week they met up once again for the woodland count. They spent two hours in the wood with the morning count and in the evening they gathered again to go into the wood. There were not nearly as many attending as in the morning, for some of the members found it rather scary in the wood at sunset. Claire had sympathy with their point of view when she heard the fox barking and the caw of the crows that very night. When it looked like the only ones that were willing to attend were the members of the quartet plus Claire and Abigail. They set off in the cars of Mr Beatty and Mrs Fisher and soon came to the edge of the wood and parked. They then ventured into the wood, this brave bunch of six amateur ornithologists.

When the first call of a fox was heard Abigail nearly jumped out of her skin. She grabbed hold of Claire's sleeve and held on. As the birds began to fly into roost, Mr Beatty photographed them with his telescopic camera, while the others counted the different types of birds hoping to spot a jackdaw, a rook or a raven. With the sound of the wind in the trees along with noise of the crickets the wood began to feel like a rather creepy place. It was then they spotted a big house in the distance which appeared to be empty, and this made things appear to be even more scary.

Having been by now sometime in the wood, Mr Beatty decided it was time to leave and everyone present breathed a sigh of relief. Just as they were setting off to the cars Claire spotted movement not too far away and heard voices. She could hear what the intruders were saying and she did not like it at all. "Get down and be quiet," she whispered, while at the same time kneeling down pulling Abigail with her.

The rest of them went to ground and spoke not a word. "Everyone back to the car and leave," ordered Mr Beatty, after using his binoculars to see what Claire had been worried about.

"I'm staying with you, Mr Beatty," whispered

Claire.

"And I'm staying with you, Claire," whispered Abigail. Claire pressed her hand to thank her. Mr Beatty was not going to argue with Claire about her staying, but he would have preferred Abigail to have gone to the car, for he had seen with his binoculars had put him on red alert. They were alone now, just the three of them. Soon Abigail saw the reason for Claire's precautions. A bunch of young children were being marched along a footpath to the eerie house not too far away. Claire counted there were twelve children, both boys and girls. A woman with a whip was in charge of them and they did what they were told. She kept them moving by swearing and cursing them.

"Slave labour!" exclaimed Mr Beatty, when it dawned on him just what was happening. "What on earth are we going to do?" They both turned and looked at Claire, and waited for an answer.

"Let's see where they are headed," said Claire. They continued along the footpath until they came to the driveway of the eerie house and turned into it, for the gate was wide open as if waiting for them. It wasn't much of a driveway for it was a rather short distance from the gates to the porch. "Let's hide in the bushes opposite the entrance to the driveway," said Claire, which they then did.

From their hiding place the three of them saw the woman in charge ring the doorbell to be answered by a small, sinister looking man, who ushered them in, counting the children as he did so. "We shall have to phone the police. This is obviously a case of child trafficking," said an enraged Mr Beatty. "Let's just phone the police and let them deal with it now. It will be pitch dark soon."

"I think we should wait awhile in case anyone else arrives," said Claire. If the police arrive and demand entry to the house, these gangsters will have time to phone their accomplices and warn them not to come." When Claire finished speaking she looked over at Mr Beatty to hear what he was going to say.

"As I said, it's getting dark, and very soon it will be pitch black. I just don't want you two girls to get frightened," said Mr Beatty, who was now really concerned about the safety of them. Unfortunately for him it turned out to be the wrong thing to say.

"I don't mind staying," said Claire.

"I don't mind either," said Abigail quite defiantly.

Mr Beatty knew he was defeated. "Very well we shall all stay," he announced, and then he phoned Mrs Fisher to let her know.

CHAPTER 57

Claire Again to the Rescue

It turned out to be a very good decision, for just a few minutes later, the headlight of a van was spotted approaching which then turned in and parked at the front porch. Claire had noted its number plate. Then a man got out and entered the house. Claire went into her backpack and took out a pair of five inch needle nose pliers.

"I'll be back in a minute," she said, and before Mr Beatty could complain she had gone. Claire ran to the van, found the valve stem on one of the tyres, removed the cap on the valve, then using her pliers turned the metal pin inside the valve to deflate the tyre. She was soon back with her friends in no time at all.

"What were you doing?" asked Abigail. When Claire told both of them they were astounded.

Then another two vans arrived and parked on either side of the porch and waited. There was now no room for any other vehicles to park inside the gates. It was then the gates closed. "I don't think any more will come now," said Claire. The others agreed. "Just one more thing to do," said Claire, and off she went once more. Her two friends watched, with the help of the light of the moon. Claire entered the wood and appeared a few minutes later dragging a tree trunk after her. She dragged it all the way up to the entrance of the driveway and set it down so it lay at the front of the gates, stretching from one pillar to the other pillar and even beyond. She then did the very same thing with two other tree trunks, before returning to her friends. "Just in case," she said. "I just had to make sure." Claire then got her camera out from her backpack and told the others to get ready with their phones.

A few minutes later, the men came out of the house each with four children which they shoved into the back of their vans. The gates were opened but the driver with the flat tyre did not get very far. He jumped out of his van, and when he spotted the flat tyre, he started shouting and swearing at the other two men sitting alone in their vans, demanding to know who had done this. Those in the other vans got out and there was almost a fist fight. "Time to phone the police now," said Claire, and brought out her phone with her new SIM card.

"Claire, let me phone instead," suggested Mr Beatty."The police will be wanting to know what you were doing in the wood at this time of day."

"It's OK. I just use this phone for a one off phone call," she said, and so saying she phoned the police using the voice of an old man who was badger watching, and told them about the plight of the children. Her two companions stared at her in amazement when they heard this voice coming from the young girl. Claire smiled over at the two and gave them a wink. "Now let's get out of here," said Claire. In no time at all they were in the car and heading down the hill.

Back at the eerie house the traffickers had spotted the tree trunks at the gate and were desperately trying to leave in their vans. They drove up to the gate, but no matter how they tried they could not move the trunks. They needed a longer run up to the gate to gain momentum to try and shift them. They then got out of their vans demanding their money back that they had paid to the gangster for the children. A fight broke out as the three men set upon the gangster. In desperation he drew his gun and killed all three.

By now Claire and her companions were well away from what was going on at the sinister house, and soon arrived outside Mrs Fisher's house where in the distance they could hear the police sirens. Before they left the car, Claire looked at her two companions. "I want you to promise me that you will never tell anyone anything you saw me doing or heard me saying." They both promised. It was then Mrs Fisher came out of her house and ushered them inside. Claire and Abigail then phoned home to say they were back at Mrs Fisher's safe and sound after counting the birds. "We were so worried about you," said Miss Willow, when the girls had ended the call. Mr Beatty then told them what had happened, after which they all bowed their heads as Mrs Fisher got to her feet to thank God for their safe return. Next they had a very nice dinner after which they split up, and Mrs Fisher showed the girls to their bedrooms. In the morning it was all over the news, not only the local news, but the whole country about the child trafficking foiled by the quick thinking of a badger watcher and a group of his friends who had blocked the escape of the child slavers using fallen tree trunks. They went on to say that three men had been killed, and the police were searching for a man and a woman, and until they were found advised the local public to stay indoors. The children were being cared for by the local council, and had been saved from working in sweatshops.

Mr Beatty now back home, bowed his head when the news bulletin was over, and thanked God they had left before the carnage had started.

CHAPTER 58

The Raven

One Saturday morning when Claire set off to walk her dogs, she spotted a young, injured raven lying in the driveway of the house, trying to move into a hiding place beside the bushes. The poor bird wasn't making much progress, so Claire bent down beside it. She saw it had a broken leg and a damaged wing, hence she gently picked the terrified bird up and returned to the servant's quarters. There her mother helped Claire place the bird into an unused little hut.

That very morning Mrs Sipps was snooping around the hen house and the old rabbit hut looking for faults to harangue Claire's mum with, and she found one. "A crow being looked after in *my* hut," she said, in a sinister voice as she ground her teeth. She immediately made her way to the kitchen to confront Claire's mum. She flung open the kitchen door and started yelling at her.

"Get that crow out of my hut," she screeched, pointing at the hut which could be seen through the window.

"It is in there because it needs the heat," replied

Claire's mum, not bothering to tell her that it was actually a raven. "It's got a broken leg and wing, and if it is ejected from the hut it will surely die of the cold." Mrs Sipps couldn't care less about the bird, for she was looking for a fight, and she thought she now had a just cause.

"Move it or you're fired," yelled Mrs Sipps, and folded her arms while she glared at Claire's mum in a threatening manner.

"Your son agreed we could keep our pets in the house or outside, and therefore the raven stays," said Claire's mum defiantly.

"You're fired," screamed Mrs Sipps. I want you, along with your stupid pets, and an imbecile of a daughter, out of my house and property. As for the crow, I suggest you deposit it in one of the wheelie bins where it rightly belongs. It's a nuisance just like you and that halfwit of a daughter of yours."

"Elijah did not think that about God's friendly raven, nor those that work in the Tower of London, where there are at all times six ravens or more," said Claire's mother.

"What have you been drinking?" asked Mrs Sipps, full of rage. It was at that moment Claire returned from her morning walk with her dogs.

"What's wrong, Mum?" she asked, when she saw the worried look on her mother's face, and Mrs Sipps standing scowling at her.

"I have been sacked and we have to leave by midday, and take the raven with us," said Claire's mum. Claire looked across the room to see Mrs

Sipps standing with arms folded. When she saw Claire looking at her she glared at the young girl, and then left the kitchen slamming the door behind her, only to return a short time later with a cheque for Claire's mum severance pay. Not for a minute did Mrs Sipps believe that Claire and her mum would leave, for there was the threat of them becoming homeless. She expected the pair of them to be soon knocking at the door of her room, begging not to be fired, with the crow now in the wheelie bin. Oh, how wrong could she be.

Claire phoned Mr Beatty and found he was at home, so off she went to see him and tell him all that had happened. "Right, you and your mum are not going to stay with that woman a moment longer than necessary. You can stay in the servants' bungalow at the back of my house as long as you want. Let's go and collect your mum and your stuff." Just a few minutes later they were driving up the hill in Mr Beatty's van.

"Don't let Mrs Sipps see your van or yourself, Mr Beatty, for we don't want her to know where we are going," said Claire, as they approached the big house. Mr Beatty drove as close to the house as he could without being seen. "I'll go and collect Mum and our belongings. We did not bring much stuff with us," said Claire.

"Make sure she does not accuse you of stealing anything," said Mr Beatty.

"Oh, I shall, I shall," said Claire, determined to do so.

CHAPTER 59
Patience Ends

Mr Beatty set about reversing his van, while Claire headed to the servants' quarters where she found her mother outside at the scullery door waiting for her. She was delighted when Claire gave her the good news, and greeted it with a huge sigh of relief.

"I just could not face another hour with that woman," said Claire's mum. It was not just the way that Mrs Sipps had treated her, but also the horrible things she had said about Claire, that had made Claire's mother so determined now to leave. "It is such a relief to have some place to go and stay now." They then collected all their belongings and brought them to the scullery, where Claire placed her phone on a shelf to record what was about to occur. Her mother would switch it on when she heard Claire return with Mrs Sipps. Claire then went to tell Mrs Sipps that they were leaving. She knocked at her door and was told to enter. Mrs Sipps had been sitting waiting for them to apologise and beg her to let them stay. That was not going to happen.

"So she has sent you here to grovel and apologise,

hoping I shall change my mind and let you stay, child," said Mrs Sipps, with a smile on her face thinking she had won the stand-off.

"We are leaving right now," Claire told her, with a defiant tone of voice, showing Mrs Sipps that she was not to be intimidated. "If you want to see what we are taking with us then come to the scullery."

"I certainly shall, child," said Mrs Sipps, as if Claire was some kind of thief.

When they got to the scullery, a place that Mrs Sipps hardly ever entered, Claire's mum showed her all the things they were taking. She then got Mrs Sipps to examine the bags she was using to place her things into. She filled the two bags with clothes and placed them outside at the scullery door next to Big Dog and Mitzy. Claire then put her mother's chair and her own chair beside the bags. Next she emptied her backpack in front of Mrs Sipps and then put the stuff back in. She had hidden her wigs under the seat of Mr Beatty's van.

"Time to leave now," said Claire's mum, as she walked to the door and turned and looked Mrs Sipps in the eye.

"Oh, you'll be back," said Mrs Sipps, while wagging a finger at her and giving her a dirty look. As they stared at each other Claire picked up her phone and went to join her mum. "Remember to take your crow with you," called out Mrs Sipps, as she slammed the scullery door shut. She then went back to her room and waited, and waited and waited.

Claire's mum set off for the van carrying the two bags with Big Dog and Mitzy at her side. Claire was right behind her carrying her mother's wooden chair in one hand, and her own with her other hand. Mr Beatty warmly greeted them and helped Claire's mum with the bags, which let Clare retrieve her wigs from under the passenger seat. Claire then ran back to collect her pets, including the raven. While they waited for Claire to return, Mr Beatty placed the bags into the back of his van, then did the same with the wooden chair. After that he tried to lift the other chair, Claire's Chair, but could not budge it.

At that moment Claire returned with Big Hen, Hoppity Hop and the raven, all in cardboard boxes, and Mr Beatty struggling to lift her chair. Claire suggested that Mr Beatty look after the boxes, and right before his eyes she lifted her chair into the back of the van. She then ran back to collect Hoppity's empty small hutch leaving Mr Beatty scratching his head wondering how Claire had managed to lift the chair and he hadn't. Then he remembered Claire lifting the tree trunks and other things she had done. He was completely awestruck and stood there looking up into the sky. "Excuse me Mr Beatty, I think we had better be on our way," he suddenly heard a voice say, as a small hand tugged at his shirt sleeve. Claire had returned along with Hoppity's hutch, and in no time at all they were heading down the hill to Mr Beatty's bungalow at the back of his mansion.

CHAPTER 60

The Painting Exhibition

On Saturday the art class had been cancelled, for there was to be an exhibition of their best paintings to be held in the town hall. The members had to hand in those paintings they wanted to exhibit. Claire had chosen paintings of her pets while her friend Emily, who was also a talented singer, had chosen her bird paintings. It happened to be that Mr Clark, apart from being an art teacher, was also the conductor of the local amateur orchestra, which he set up using money from Sir Robert Buchanan's charity for setting up orchestras throughout the country. When he had the time, Sir Robert would visit those orchestras his charity had helped, to find out how they were progressing. Well it was now the turn of Mr Clark's orchestra to have a visit from Sir Robert which had been arranged a month ago. The art exhibition was to be held, on the very same day as Sir Robert's visit, at the same time, in the town hall.

Now on her way to the exhibition Claire spotted a certain Mrs Amber, who ran the only *Vets Vets Vets* charity shop in the town. Claire had become a volunteer helper in the back of the shop whenever she could. She soon caught up with the middle aged lady. "Hello, Mrs Amber," said Claire, "are you going to the painting exhibition in the town hall?"

"No, I'm not, Claire," answered Mrs Amber, and said nothing more until they came to the town hall and entered. "Goodbye, Claire," said Mrs Amber, as she headed off to a large room in the hall.

"Goodbye Mrs Amber," said Claire, "and call into the painting exhibition before you leave, and I shall show you my paintings."

When Claire entered through the door into the painting exhibition, she found all the paintings had already been hung by those who help run the charity, mostly former pupils of Mr Clark. Claire's paintings were hung close to Emily's paintings of garden birds. Claire had chosen just to hang paintings of her pets.

A short time after the start, Claire suddenly heard an orchestra tuning up in the large room, and started to play parts of Tchaikovsky's first piano concerto. She kept wondering what Mr Clark was up to, for she knew that it was no coincidence that the orchestra were meeting at the same time as the art exhibition, which was strange as the orchestra always met on Saturday afternoon.

It was about half past eleven when the orchestra stopped rehearsing, and a short time later the members of the orchestra entered the exhibition and went round looking at the paintings. Then the door opened and in came Mr Clark and Mrs

Amber, along with a tall handsome young man, who just happened to be Sir Robert Buchanan. "A coincidence! Most definitely not," said Claire, and smiled.

The three of them had been discussing with Sir Robert Buchanan the possibility of him conducting the local orchestra in a charity event to raise money for *VetsVetsVets,* and the charity, *Your Orchestra,* which helped the setting up of new orchestras.

Mr Clark then excused himself and went looking for Claire in the crowded hall. Meanwhile, Sir Robert was left looking at the paintings along with Mrs Amber, when suddenly he noticed three paintings that caught his eye. He excused himself and walked over to have a closer look at them. Some memory was churning away in his head, for he was sure he had seen the hen and the rabbit somewhere before. Who painted these?" he asked.

CHAPTER 61
A Surprise for Sir Robert

"It was I," came the reply from a small quiet voice. He quickly turned around to find a young girl with a big smile on her face gazing up at him.

"I might have known!" he exclaimed quietly, for he could see that Claire did not want the others in the room to hear what was being said, while doing his best not to start bursting out laughing. "You have often shown me photos of these two, Hoppity Hop and Big Hen. "It's nice to see you once more, but how did you know I would be here today?"

"I didn't," said Claire, as she shrugged her shoulders and spread out her hands. Claire then introduced Emily to Sir Robert.

"Now that I have met you again, Claire," said Sir Robert, "I can now understand why just an hour ago, Mr Clark asked if I could come back in a fortnight and conduct Tchaikovsky's first. I told him I would think about it. He only needed to have mentioned your name and I would have instantly accepted his invitation. I'm sure I can fit it into my busy schedules. "

"Now that *is* interesting," said Claire. "Would you

be free that day Emily?" asked Claire.

"Yes," said Emily, while wondering why Claire had asked her the question

Before anything else could be said the voice of Mrs Amber sounded. "Now Claire, you can't monopolise Sir Robert Buchanan. Others are dying to meet you Sir Robert," and so saying she took him by the arm and led him away. As he was being pulled along he turned his head and winked at Claire, who smiled and raised her eyes to the ceiling. However, Sir Robert did manage to convince Mrs Amber that he and Claire were old acquaintances, so they returned and joined Claire and Emily. Next to appear was Mr Clark. "Really Mr Clark," said Claire, as if she was talking to an errant child of five, "that was very naughty of you, not telling me of Sir Robert's visit." When she had finished wagging her finger at him, they all smiled.

It was then the town clock struck twelve, so it was time for the exhibition to end. Mr Clark thanked all who had participated and asked them to take their paintings home with them. Sir Robert went to help Claire remove her paintings. He did not start right away taking them down, but stood and admired them as if he was lost in wonder. "Are these your pets too?" he asked Claire, pointing to the painting of Big Dog and Mitzy together.

"Yes they are," replied Claire, hoping he liked it.

"It's a beautiful painting, like all the others. What are your dogs' names?" he asked, but Claire was interrupted by Sir Robert before Claire could answer. "No, don't tell me. Are they by any chance, Big Dog and Wee Dog?" He looked at Claire waiting for her answer.

"I do wonder what made you think of these names Sir Robert, but you are just half correct," answered Claire, with a big smile. "That's Big Dog and Mitzy that you're looking at." They placed the paintings in a shopping bag and returned to Mr Clark and Mrs Amber, who were keen to engage Sir Robert in conversation.

CHAPTER 62

The Big Question

The time had now arrived to ask Sir Robert the big question, so Mr Clark dutifully stepped up and asked.

"Before you have to leave, Sir Robert, we were wondering, now that you have heard our orchestra playing, if you had made up your mind about what Mrs Amber and myself were discussing with you?"

"Oh yes, I have now made up my mind if only I can persuade a certain young girl to be the pianist?"

"And who would that be?" asked Mrs Amber, excited at the prospect of it going ahead.

"Why none other than Claire, who is standing next to us all," answered Sir Robert. Mrs Amber was not amused, thinking it was some type of silly joke, while on the other hand Mr Clark was delighted.

"Claire, will you play the piano in Tchaikovsky's first piano concerto for us, on Saturday afternoon, a fortnight from today?" asked Sir Robert, who already knew the answer. "The profits will be shared equally with our charities."

"I would be delighted to," answered Claire, "but

I have a few suggestions to make. Number one is that Sir Robert accepts as a gift these three paintings of mine," and so saying she handed them to him. "I also suggest that we have some local singers at the concert, for that will bring in more of the locals. I nominate Emily and our local church choir." Emily smiled and now saw the relevance of being asked if she was free on that date, and of course was delighted that she would be taking part. "And almost finally I suggest Mr Clark is the host of the concert and Sir Robert and Mrs Amber make speeches at the close of the concert. As for the printing of the tickets, please don't put my name on it, for I doubt if any people here have heard of me. Keep it as a mystery who will be the pianist." Claire looked at Sir Robert with her big pleading eyes. What else could he do but accept her suggestions.

Mr Clark had been worried that there could be a low turnout for the concerto, so he was very pleased with Claire's suggestions. "Sir Robert says yes," cried Mr Clark, to the members of the orchestra who had been patiently waiting for the result of negotiations. There was a huge cheer from the members for they would now be conducted by the world famous Sir Robert Buchanan.

"And thank you for your paintings, Claire," said Sir Robert, as he looked at them once again. "I shall hang them in my study when I get back home tonight. Now I have to depart, for I have to visit some other orchestras this very afternoon. I hope to meet you all again two weeks from today. He started to leave, but then suddenly stopped and looked at Claire. "I do hope your mother will get time off to come to the concert Claire, for I would love to meet her again." He then left leaving Mrs Amber standing staring, wondering who exactly this young girl Claire was. Then it dawned upon her.

"It's Claire!" she exclaimed out loud, for she had often read about her in the charities in house news sheets. Some people in the hall gave her a funny look.

CHAPTER 63

Selling Tickets

Soon the tickets had been printed and Claire handed her allocation to sell. There were only two names on the ticket, one being Sir Robert Buchanan, and the other being Tchaikovsky. Claire's name did not appear for it was left as a mystery as to who the pianist would be. She had also been given the task of finding others to perform beside Emily, for on the ticket it stated that local singers would perform.

The first person Claire decided she would try to partake in the concert was Mrs Hay. One day on her way home from school, she called in at Mrs Hay's house and was invited into the sitting room, where sat Miss Willow who also was visiting Mrs Hay. Claire got down to business right away. She told them about the upcoming concert and then asked the big question that was on her mind, while thinking they would be all for her proposal. "Would you be willing to help us out, and have the Church choir sing at the concert in the town hall?"

The two ladies gasped in horror at the suggestion, so Claire gave them a look that demanded some sort of explanation.

"If it had been anywhere else but the town hall, we would have accepted your invitation for our choir to sing, but, oh no Claire, not in that place," said Mrs Hay, while shaking her head and uttering one mighty sigh. Claire just could not understand why, so Miss Willow decided to shine some light on the situation.

"You see Claire, we have been there before at the town hall. The choir sang and we got booed and rotten fruit and eggs thrown at us by a group of thugs. I have learnt from others that they too have gone through such humiliation. The rumour is that someone pays them to do that."

"We are sorry, Claire, but we just can't participate in your concert," said Mrs Hay. "I'm sure Mr Clark will probably be completely unaware of what could happen. We have been to hear his orchestra several times, but it has always been in smaller halls. He must be thinking that the name of Sir Robert will draw a big crowd of people, but it will also bring in that group of thugs who seem to haunt the town hall."

"Now I understand," said Claire. "Would you then

like to buy a ticket to the concert?" asked Claire, already knowing what their answers would be. They both just shook their heads. Claire never told them that Emily and herself would be appearing at the concert, for she felt that would put pressure on the two retired ladies, which she certainly did not want to do. "I better be on my way now," said Claire. "Thanks for telling me about these thugs," and off she went.

CHAPTER 64

Try Again

Claire then paid a visit to Mrs Fisher's house where she found Mrs Fisher working in her front garden. Claire told Mrs Fisher all about the upcoming concert in the town hall and then asked her if she would like to buy a ticket, which Claire expected her to say no, which she did. Claire had to ask her anyway for she might have felt rejected if she had been the only one in the quartet not to be asked. "Who else is in the concert apart from Sir Robert?" asked Mrs Fisher.

"Emily will be singing and I shall be playing the piano," answered Claire, having wished that Mrs Fisher had not asked the question.

"Oh, I never knew that they have asked you to accompany Emily on the piano," said Mrs Fisher, looking quite surprised, but at the same time not at all pleased that the best that could be found to play the piano, was a young girl like Claire. "You better find some place to practise. You don't want to make a fool of yourself, do you?"

"Oh no!" cried Claire. "The thing is I was never allowed to play the piano when we were staying in the Big House. Mrs Sipps was adamant about that," said Claire, with a sigh. Claire then looked Mrs Fisher up and down wondering if she should request a favour from her. She did ask even though in her heart she knew it would be in vain. "I was wondering if you would please let me practise on your grand piano, Mrs Fisher?" Claire really wanted to rehearse, and was not just taking it for granted that she could play Tchaikovsky without practising.

"Oh, I could never permit you to play on my grand," said Mrs Fisher, quite shocked that Claire had even asked the question. It is a very delicate instrument, Claire, and worth a lot of money."

"I understand," said Claire, who was looking rather disappointed, not because of being turned down, but by the hard heartedness of Mrs Fisher.

Claire then headed for home which was the bungalow at the back of Mr Beatty's mansion. She was hoping to meet Mr Beatty, the fourth member of the quartet, in his garden and she was not disappointed, for he was working on his beehives. Claire also told him all about the concert, including the thugs. He too was surprised to hear that Claire was taking part in the concert, but her part in it was a secret. Claire then offered to sell him a ticket, again expecting him to turn down the offer. "Oh, I shall take ten," said Mr Beatty, "and sell the other nine to my friends and fellow beekeepers."

Claire looked surprised and Mr Beatty noticed it. "Did you try to sell tickets to the rest of the quartet, Claire?" asked Mr Beatty.

"Yes, but they did not want to go," said Claire, doing her best not to tell Mr Beatty that the behaviour of the thugs had frightened them off.

"I understand, for I was there when it happened and I don't blame them, Claire," said Mr Beatty. "These town hall gangs would scare off most people, but not us beekeepers. If we can face a swarm of bees we sure ain't afraid of a group of silly big youths. We'll be there at the concert. Don't you worry."

"I'm trying to find people to partake in the concert. Do you know of anyone who could partake, Mr Beatty?" asked Claire.

"Oh yes,, I know some who would be delighted to perform at the town hall," said Mr Beatty, with a mischief twinkle in his eyes.

"Can you tell me who it is?" asked Claire.

"It is I. All I need to know is when you want me for rehearsal, and I'll be there."

"And what is it you will be doing, Mr Beatty?" asked Claire, who was dying to find out.

"If you tell me what you'll be doing then I shall tell you what I shall be doing," he answered. They both had to laugh.

CHAPTER 65
Courageous Ruth

A few days later, on her way home from school, with her friends Abigail and Ruth, they met Mrs Hay working in her front garden. How are you getting on Claire selling your tickets?" called out Mrs Hay

"So, so," answered Claire, thinking of those tickets that she had sold to Mr Beatty.

"Good for you Claire," remarked Mrs Hay, and continued looking after her plants.

"What's this about a concert?" asked Abigail, not being too pleased that she had not been offered a ticket. Now Claire had not told them about the concert as she thought it was far too dangerous for them to attend. She explained to them her reason the best she could.

"Rubbish," said Abigail. "I'm not letting a group of thugs stop me from going to see my friend on stage. I'll take a ticket. What about you Ruth?"

"I want to go too," she said. "I enjoyed the one in the church hall." Tickets had been printed for children, and they were not expensive, for one of the aims of the charities was to promote their work among children. For some reason or another, Claire was glad that Abigail and Ruth had bought the tickets. She then signed the back of the ticket which would let them sit in the front row. Next day at school Claire did the very same thing for her friend Gwen.

Claire had made a list of those she would try and sell tickets to. There was just now one left on the list who had to be asked and that was Mrs Sipps. She had prayed about the situation and was now determined to visit Mrs Sipps. The fact that Ruth was not letting bullies prevent her attending the concert, also greatly encouraged Claire to visit the cantankerous Mrs Sipps. "If Ruth can face the bullies then surely I can face Mrs Sipps," said Claire to herself, so off went Claire up the hill and along the driveway to visit the Big House.

When she arrived she rang the bell at the front porch and waited. As no one came to the door Claire thought it would be best now to leave. She had just wanted to be kind to Mrs Sipps and had hoped that some of that kindness would rub off onto Mrs Sipps. As Claire stepped down from the porch, and had made a few steps on her homeward journey, suddenly an upstairs window flew open and out popped the head of Mrs Sipps. "What do you want?" she shouted out, and then looking down she spotted Claire. "Oh it's you," she cried.

"Mrs Sipps, would you like to buy a ticket for Tchaikovsky's first piano concerto in the town hall, conducted by Sir Robert Buchanan," shouted

Claire up to the open window. "There will also be singing by locals and I shall be accompanying one of them on the piano. I think you may enjoy it."

"Just a minute, Claire. I shall come down and see you," she said, in what was now a complete change of tone in her voice, a rather pleasant tone, which put Claire into a state of alert. Claire kept watching the empty window and not the door, as she waited for Mrs Sipps' return. Suddenly it seemed to Claire that a bucket of water came flying out of the open window aimed at her. She easily avoided getting soaked, but if she had been watching the door to see who was coming, she would have been drenched. Nevertheless, Claire yelled out as if Mrs Sipps had scored a bull's eye. Just as the window was being pulled closed, Claire, just for a fraction of a second, saw a large vase in the other hand of the culprit. Claire simply shook off the few drops of water that had landed on her shoes and left. "I wonder if she was trying to kill me," she asked a crow, watching her while perched on a branch of a high tree. "I ask you because you must have had a lot of attempts at people trying to kill you." It made several grating caws then flew off.

CHAPTER 66
The Day of the Concert

Rehearsals for the concert, even without Sir Robert Buchanan being present, went well for all those in the orchestra. The orchestra met in the hall, while Emily and Mr Beatty met in different places at different times. Emily had chosen Claire as her accompanist, while Mr Beatty had chosen one of his friends. When Claire found out that the orchestra had been rehearsing many weeks before without a virtuoso pianist, she approached Mr Clark with a big smile on her face. "Mr Clark," she said, in a voice that was going to give him a telling off, "what would you have done if I had rejected your proposal to play the piano?"

"It was irresistible. Wasn't it?" asked Mr Clark. They both laughed.

The day of the concert soon arrived. For Sir Robert it would be a very busy day, as he had lots of other commitments to fulfil apart from that of conducting the Concerto with Claire. He had promised to be there with Claire and he kept his promise. He had a chat with the orchestra, telling them he was looking forward to conducting, and was sure the Concerto would be a great success. However, some of the audience who would be attending had other ideas. Now Claire knew all about the town hall gangs having learnt a lot from Mr Beatty. Mr Beatty and his friends had volunteered to collect the tickets at the door before the concert started. The doors would be closed five minutes before the start of the concert so that the audience could settle in. Now Claire had made plans with Mr Beatty as to what had to be done if there was any disturbances or continued booing and disruption in the foyer or in the hall, while the show was going on. "It's just a precaution, Mr Beatty," said Claire, but it turned out to be a very wise precaution indeed.

Just before the opening of the doors, which was half an hour before the concert would begin, Claire went down to the door to help Mr Beatty and his friends. At the appointed time the doors opened and people started to enter. Their tickets were checked and then they were shown into the hall by other volunteers. Things went well until a group of five thugs were getting their tickets checked. By their appearances, they just did not look like they were there to enjoy the music. They were all carrying a plastic bag which was a red alert for Mr Beatty and his friends. Their tickets were taken then they were told to open their bags, which were found to contain rotten fruit and eggs. They were given their money back and were told to leave. At this point they would have pushed Mr Beatty aside, but when they saw his friends step up to the mark, like all bullies, they just slunk away.

As time went by groups of other dodgy looking people entered, but they had their tickets and were allowed to enter the hall. Then just before the doors were to be shut, in came a group of twenty youths all without a ticket. They were big enough and looked vicious enough to push aside Mr Beatty's group and force their way into the auditorium. It was then, Claire, who had been keeping herself in the shadows, stepped forward ready to act, after saying an emergency prayer. "Get out of my way you old fool," shouted the leader of the gang in Mr Beatty's face. "We're going in whether you like it or not."

"Oh no, you're not," came the voice of a young girl who had slipped into the space between Mr Beatty and the thug. "Just leave," she ordered, as she looked up into the cruel eyes of the bully. He could not believe what he had just heard coming from this young girl. He seemed to be mesmerised by her and just stared and stared at her. When he recovered his senses he became very aggressive and swore at Claire. This was not good enough for Claire. She wanted him to strike out at her, for she believed she could take him out. "Just leave you foul-mouthed boy."

That was all it took, for he completely lost it and thrust out his hand to push her into Mr Beatty, and knock both to the ground, but that just did not happen. Claire saw his large outstretched hand approaching her in slow motion, grabbed it and pulled it with all her might, and got herself out of the way as this large hunk of a body landed face down slithering across the polished floor of the entrance hall. When he stopped he got to his feet and rushed at Claire with his arms flapping away and his hands clenched ready to inflict as much harm as he could on the young girl.

"They never learn," said Claire to herself, as he drew closer and closer to Claire. She simply acted as she had done a few seconds before and sent him once again sliding face down along the floor. She ran up to him and placed her foot on his back so he could not rise. The members of his gang in no way wanted to be associated with a leader that had just been humiliated by a little girl, or any girl as a matter of fact. One by one they left, leaving Claire alone to deal with what to them was their fallen disgraced leader, that they now wanted nothing to do with. Claire took her foot from off his back, and watched him as he got up and left.

The fall of the bully had lasted just a few seconds, and as much as Mr Beatty and his friends had wanted to help, it had been made almost impossible by the quick actions of Claire. The doors were then shut and the concert was about to start in five minutes. "Please don't tell anyone what just happened," said Claire," for it may put my life in danger," and off she went to get ready for the show.

CHAPTER 67
The Performance

The concert began with Emily walking onto the front of the stage, with the curtain closed behind her. The microphone was at the centre of the stage and there she sang *Flow Gently, Sweet Afton,* accompanied by a pianist, who just happened to be Claire, at the side of the stage. That was followed by Mr Beatty singing *On the Road to Mandalay,* accompanied by his friend on the piano. Both received a warm round of applause, which surprised Mr Beatty for just a few seconds, who was expecting to be booed, and then he remembered the twenty thugs that Claire had sent on their way. Mr Beatty then announced that the next event would be Sir Robert Buchanan conducting the local orchestra in Tchaikovsky's piano concerto number one. He then started to leave.

As he left the stage he glanced at the audience

and spotted groups of thugs sitting together, all looking smug and menacing. They would have booed him and Emily, but they thought the gang of twenty were present and they would do the booing. "The thugs by now have probably worked out that the gang of twenty were not going to appear, so it was up to them to start the booing and ruin the concerto," said Mr Beatty to himself. "They are only here to cause trouble." He was soon to be proved right.

The microphone was then removed from the stage and the curtain was raised revealing the whole orchestra with the grand piano right at the front at the centre of the stage with the podium for the conductor close by. Everybody knew who the conductor would be, but who the pianist would be was still a mystery. The hall was actually packed full, for most of the audience had come to see the famous Sir Robert Buchanan. The tickets had not been expensive and were a bargain compared to the price they would have to pay in the big cities. Most of the audience were expecting the pianist to be someone famous, and were hoping it would be one of their favourites. They were going to be in for a big disappointment when Claire walked on to the stage.

When the side door to the stage opened and in walked Claire, the thugs in the crowd seemed to go crazy. They started booing and shouting with all their might. They enjoyed it only wishing they had done the same when Emily and Mr Beatty had appeared. A few paces behind Claire came Sir Robert, with baton in hand. He appeared to be shocked with the abuse Claire was receiving, whereas to Claire it was like water off a duck's back.

As usual she bowed to the audience, shook hands with the first violinist and sat down at the piano and looked around. There in the front row was her mother sitting next to Abigail and her little sister Ruth, who Claire was expecting to see. She gave them a little wave and then looked to see who else was there in the front row. To her surprise, sitting in the front row were the three ladies of the quartet, who had been persuaded by Mr Beatty to attend. All of them had a worried look on their face, all three believing Claire had taken a funny turn, and somehow had convinced Sir Robert to believe that she was some sort of great pianist.

Sir Robert was now on the podium waiting to start once the uproar had ceased. The music lovers soon calmed down, but the groups of thugs kept at it, determined to close down the event. Realising that, Claire rose from the piano stool and walked to the centre of the stage, to the very edge of it. She raised her hands and told the thugs to be quiet, and they actually obeyed, to the surprise of the rest of the audience. The truth had dawned on Claire that these thugs, along with the other twenty, had been paid to disrupt the proceedings. She could only think of one person who would do that to her.

CHAPTER 68

Claire takes Control

The thugs stared at her waiting to hear what this little girl standing alone right on the edge in the middle of the stage was going to say. Claire opened her mouth and spoke. "If you want your money back, you simply have to go to the door and the door keepers will reimburse you." Claire had arranged all this with Mr Beatty and his friends before the doors had opened. She had mentioned the word money twice, for she was sure that that was all they were interested in, probably having been paid to disrupt the concert. "The rest of you can leave later and collect your money once they have gone." With the words of money, money, money, ringing in their years they got up and left.

When all the thugs had departed she then spoke to the audience, most of whom were amazed at what had just happened. A young girl, with the voice of authority and without a microphone, had calmed down the thugs and had persuaded them to leave. It all seemed quite astonishing to their minds. "All I ask now is that you listen to the music, but if you want your money back now, I shall give it to you," and she took out a bundle of notes from her pocket and held it up for all to see. The audience were becoming more and more fascinated by Claire by the minute, so that the vast majority of them now had no intention of leaving. Nevertheless, there is always one who wants to be different to draw attention to themselves. Such a person got up from his seat and spoke.

"I have sat here having to listen to a couple of rubbish singers, waiting to see who the pianist will be, only to find out it is you. I certainly want my money back," he said, waiting for the applause that he felt was due to him, but the rest of the audience wanted nothing to do with him.

"Here's your ticket money," said Claire, as she took it from the bundle and stretched out her hand holding the money for him to come and collect.

"You can keep your money," shouted the young man, and stormed out of the hall. With him now gone, Claire looked around the hall and found no one else wanting to leave. Once again she waved, just a little wave, to her mother and friends in the front row before returning to the piano stool. She smiled up at Sir Robert and waited for him to give the signal to start. Sir Robert glanced over at Claire, she nodded, so he raised his baton and the orchestra started to play, followed by Claire a few moments later.

The orchestra was under great pressure to perform the best they could and they did not let themselves down. Claire's performance was outstanding for she wanted to send a message to the town hall gangs that they would not be bullied. As they neared the end of the concerto, Claire kept looking over at Sir Robert to see if he was going to increase the tempo as he had done in the past with Claire. Sir Robert had full confidence in Claire and the orchestra and kept them on the race to the finish. At the end Claire did finish with a great flourish, and then rested on the keyboard. It was only a few seconds later that the audience started to clap and cheer, but it seemed much longer, not only for Claire, but also for the orchestra and the conductor. The audience had spoken.

The Concerto had been a great success. The audience kept on cheering and clapping when Claire rose and went over to shake hands with Sir Robert, and the leading violinist. She then turned round to face the orchestra and clapped for in her mind they were the heroes of the day. It was then Sir Robert left the podium, and when facing the orchestra, he raised both hands into the air, with his right hand still clutching his baton. The orchestra rose to receive the well deserved applause. Then Sir Robert went over to Claire, and with both facing the audience he raised her hand in his into the air and then both took a bow. The curtain then was drawn and they were hidden from view. On to the front of the stage then came Mrs Amber and Mr Clark to tell the audience about their charities and how their ticket money would be spent.

The hall then started to empty so Claire went down to the front row and invited all her friends and her mother to come to the back of the stage to meet Sir Robert. He was delighted to meet Claire's mother and had a little chat with her. He shook hands with them all and was very complimentary to Emily and Mr Beatty, regarding their singing. Sir Robert had to leave, for he had another appointment to keep. As he left Claire and Mr Beatty accompanied him to the door which was being guarded by Mr Beatty's friends. "I did enjoy that," he said to Claire, as he stood at the door.

"So did I," said Claire."

"Perhaps in the future the Royal Albert Hall?" suggested Sir Robert, with a twinkle in his eye. They both just had to laugh. Sir Robert's chauffeur then accompanied him to his car. He opened the back door of the car for Sir Robert Buchanan, as he turned and waved goodbye.

CHAPTER 69
Revenge

Claire knew that there would be consequences of having stood up to the now ex-leader of what Claire had named the *Twenty's Plenty* gang. She was well prepared. She knew the ex-leader would be licking his wounds, getting more and more angry day by day. "He probably wants to kill me by now," said Claire to herself. "Knowing what has been happening recently I think he will hire an attack dog to do his dirty work." Sure enough it did not take long for the revenge on Claire to be attempted. A few days after the concert, when Claire was on her way home from school, after saying goodbye to Abigail and Ruth, the ex-leader made his move.

As Claire was walking alone along a street, she suddenly noticed the ex-leader walking in the opposite direction on the other side of the road, with a dog on a leash. He had hired the dog for the day which had cost him a lot of money, for this was not just an ordinary attack dog, but it was also a rabid dog, which meant it was affected by rabies. It was very dangerous indeed.

The dog wasn't all that big, but in Claire's eyes it looked like it could be dangerous. Claire did not believe that it was some sort of coincidence that he was there. She was proven to be correct, for when he had just passed her, she turned round as he was about to bend down and release the dog, but realising Claire was watching he just dropped the lead. "Kill," he cried out, in such a commanding voice, that he left the dog in no doubt as to what its mission was. Off it went racing across the road and then leaping in the air at the target of Claire's throat. Claire had not budged from the spot, but stood there waiting to deal with the dog, which made the thug believe she was frozen to the spot with fear.

Claire watched in slow motion, as the dog bared its teeth ready to sink deep into her throat. She easily sidestepped the killer dog, while at the same time managing to grab hold of its lead. She then ran away from the scene dragging the dog along with her on a very short leash. From her pocket she removed a wig and put it on which made her look like an entirely different girl. Claire ran along almost deserted streets until she came to a crossroad on a hill. The street going uphill was the one she chose to enter. There she tied the dog to a thin sign poll, using the lead and leaving it on a very short leash, so it could not leap out and attack someone. Next Claire walked briskly up the gently sloping hill until she came to a high wall with a van parked next to it. There she turned round to see what was happening to the dog which was now barking very loudly. The street was still deserted, but then several people came out of their houses to see what was going on. Some seemed to be taking photos, while others were phoning. "I hope they are phoning the police," said Claire to herself, for it was her plan that the police would come and take the dog. However, her plan did not quite work out the way she had hoped. Most of the spectators then went back inside, but some stayed recording what was happening on their phones.

CHAPTER 70

The Vicious Attack

The ex-gang leader had been on his way home when he heard the barking of a dog in the distance, and thought it may be his, so he set off to find it. When he arrived at the crossroads he immediately spotted his dog tied to the post. "You stupid dog," he shouted, or words to that effect. "I told you to kill her, didn't I? I had better take you back to where I got you," and on saying this he bent down to untie the dog from the post. It was then the dog started howling, and once again people left their house to see what was happening. He swore and swore at it partly because he was having great difficulty untying it from the post, having already spent several minutes trying to undo the knot, and partly because he was fed up with the poor creature.

It was then the dog bit him several times, so he got to his feet and glared down at the dog with pure hatred, which grew stronger every second. It was at this point he lost it all together and kicked the dog, but not before it had bitten him several more times. The dog howled this time with pain. Claire set off so as to stop him, but she released she was just too late for he had now stamped on its head. The howling had stopped and the dog was dead. There was now a deadly quiet, but that only lasted a short time for the sound of a distant police siren was now heard. It was like the sound of a starting pistol to him, so he quickly fled the scene of the crime. He had panicked and had no idea that the howling of the dog had brought the neighbours out into their gardens, once again with their smartphones. The sound of the sirens had not only set the thug off in retreat, but it caused most of them to return back inside their homes, for they did not want to get involved with the police. Claire now left knowing that what had just occurred would very likely appear on social media, but she never expected that it would go viral, which indeed happened. A youth, who could easily be identified kicking a dog to death, was a really shocking thing to happen.

When Claire reached home about half an hour later than her usual time, she was met by Mr

Beatty who was working in his garden. "I was worried about you, Claire," he told her. Claire gazed at him with a puzzled look on her face. Mr Beatty now felt he had to give her some sort of explanation. "I was worried because the thug we met at the concert would be looking for revenge."

"There is no need for you to worry about that any more, Mr Beatty. You can have a good night's sleep tonight," said Claire, and off she went leaving Mr Beatty once more completely dumbfounded. That very evening videos of the demise of the dog were all over social media. In her nightly prayers, Claire once again thanked God for his sovereign protection.

In the morning, when Mr Beatty switched on the news he found there was a picture of a young man that the police wanted to interview. Mr Beatty immediately recognised him as the ex-leader of the town hall gang. He then went on to social media and saw the videos of the cruel behaviour of the thug. He also recognised the crossroads, and the street where the incident took place. It only took him a few minutes to work out what had happened. It was his eureka moment, as he jumped up from his chair. "So that's why Claire was late home from school yesterday," he cried. "Who exactly is this young girl?" he asked himself, as he sank back down into his chair to rest.

Later that day there was a police message which announced that the dog had been affected by rabies. It went on to say that the youth was in great danger and should contact the police immediately. The youth was found twelve days later, but he had waited too long for treatment. He was now facing a slow, painful death. When the other attack dog owners' realised just how dangerous rabies was they got rid of their dogs. From then on there were no more planned dog attacks in the town. Claire' prayer on the subject had been answered.

CHAPTER 71

Time to Leave

Now things were happening back in the mansion where Claire's mum used to work for the Goodyards. Mrs Toeser along with her husband had been relocated, after having failed terribly in their new job. They had been replaced by a married couple and their family, who were now looking for help in running the house. They had contacted Mrs Goodyard for advice, who, without hesitation, suggested that they hire Claire's mum, Mrs Low and Bella.

It so happened that on that day, Mrs Flowers went to welcome them to their new home, for they were almost neighbours. She learnt that they were looking for Claire's mum, Mrs Low and Bella, so Mrs Flowers told them where they could be found, and after meetings and interviews it was agreed that the three would start on Friday, for that would be when Mrs Low and Bella were free to start.

This also gave Claire time to say goodbye to all of her friends. Of course, Claire's friends were all sad when they heard the news of her approaching departure, but glad her mother now had a job.

When she looked back at her time spent in this suburb of the town, she thought of Mrs Sipps alone now, in that big house of hers. Claire and her mum had tried to win her over with kindness and prayer, but it was not to be. Claire thought of all the lives that had been lost just because of their hatred for her. She had ceased hating people the day she was saved, and had accepted the Lord Jesus Christ as her Saviour. She was now filled with the fruit of the Spirit, namely love, joy, peace, patience, kindness, goodness, faith, meekness and self-control. The word hate was not on the list.

She thought also of all the people that she had managed to help, even some in insignificant ways, but to Claire it was like sprinkling a little yeast among the dough. There was for example Sandy, who was back in school hoping one day to be allowed to study to be a doctor.

The day of departure soon arrived. Early in the morning, Sid arrived in his van and they had breakfast together. He had been booked for other jobs that day, but he had managed to fit them in. Soon the van was loaded with their modest belongings along with Claire's Chair and her pets which now included the raven. Mr Beatty gave them a box of jars of honey, and reminded them to brush their teeth after using it.

Claire had said her goodbyes the day before to all her friends, for she did not want them to miss school. Only the members of the quartet came to see her off along with Abigail and Ruth. It was a big surprise to Claire when the two girls appeared, for it was a school day. The ladies of the quartet told Claire that they would make sure the two girls arrived in time. The three ladies had brought some home baking, while Abigail and Ruth had each made a card to thank Claire for all that she had done for them. Claire gave all her friends her super hug, and asked the quartet to look after the two girls. "I know you would do it anyway, whether I asked or not, but I just wanted Abigail and Ruth to know we all will be thinking and praying for them. Remember that His eye is on the sparrow." Mr Beatty then prayed they would have a safe journey to their new home.

All they had to do now was to leave. Claire's mum thanked Mr Beatty for all his help and friendship, then climbed into the passenger seat of the van, followed by Claire. The door was closed, and they moved off slowly down the driveway of the mansion. Claire put her head out of the window and saw Abigail and Ruth with tears in their eyes, and the members of the quartet looking quite sad as they stood waving. Tears were forming in Claire's eyes as she waved back.

When they came to the garden gate they turned into the cul-de-sac, and slowly moved along to the entrance. "Stop," Claire suddenly cried. They stopped; Claire opened the door, jumped out of the van and started running as fast as she could towards a young girl who had just entered the cul-de-sac and was running towards Claire. They met and gave each other a super hug. The van drew up next to them and Sid opened the door. "It's Gwen," cried Claire. Claire's mum looked out and saw the two friends standing next to each other, both with a big smile on their face.

"Bring your friend Gwen into the van and we can take her to where she wants," said Sid. "There is room enough for two." They got in and sat down, then Sid headed toward the school.

"I am afraid I have not brought you anything," said Gwen, when she saw the two cards lying on the seat.

"That is not quite true, Gwen. "You brought the sweetest gift of all, a friend's smile." Gwen blushed and smiled again.

All too soon they arrived near the school and Gwen got out. "By the way Gwen, how did you find out where and when we were leaving?" asked Claire. Gwen just tapped the side of her nose twice with her forefinger and smiled. "One day Gwen you will be tapping out notes on a grand piano at a Tchaikovsky concerto using that finger, so take care of it."

"Oh I shall," said Gwen. They both smiled.

"Bye, Gwen," said Claire.

"Bye, Claire," said Gwen.

The door was shut and Sid slowly drove away with the two friends still smiling. "Now that is unusual," thought Claire's mum and also smiled.

Soon they were on the road heading back to the place where they used to work. What was the future going to be like for this mother and her young daughter? Well, that is another story altogether.

Printed in Great Britain
by Amazon